After years of fighting Apaches and becoming the best scout in Texas Tye has become one of the best U.S. Marshals in the State. He has brought in some of the worse outlaws in the State, some alive and a few dead. Now he faces his toughest challenge, bringing in Jeb Summers better known as El Diablo or The Devil as he was known in Mexico.

Jeb was a breed born of an Apache woman and a white man. He married an Apache and lived with them for several years after his parents were killed. When the Mexicans raided his camp while he and the other men were away hunting they raped and killed his wife and his two children. He set out on a vengeful trail and it mattered not whether the victims were white, Mexican, or man or woman. He killed with a knife for the most part and cutting the victims throat was his trademark.

Tye, along with fellow deputy and friend Sam Jenkins had been ordered to track this killer down and bring him in dead or alive and it didn't matter which, just so he was caught. This proved a lot easier said than done.

McMillan

El Diablo

Chapter One

It was almost midnight and the alley between the Double Ace Saloon and Harpers General Store was as dark as sin. A shadow moved within the darkness holding close to the wall of the saloon. A man came out of the saloon and stood between the two buildings rolling himself a smoke. The man in the shadows, his pulse quickening, excitement building within, silently moved behind the man. The man must have sensed something or heard something that made him turn his head to look behind him. As he turned his head to look into the darkness the only thing he saw was the glint from the glow of the kerosene street lamp on something shiny. It was the last thing he saw as the blade cut deep across his throat. As the cowboy stood holding his throat choking on his blood that was pouring out between his fingers the killer caught him by the shoulder and jerked him into the darkness of the alley. The killer stood over the man breathing hard and feeling a sense of deep satisfaction. Gradually, his breathing came back to normal and after cutting off the ears of the dead man he walked out of the darkness of the alley to where his horse had been tied just outside of town and slowly rode away toward his camp.

"Get the dang Sheriff," a man hollered to no one in particular, and then he repeated, "Damn, can someone get Sheriff Teague." A small crowd had gathered in the alley between the Double Ace Saloon and Harpers Hardware store staring at the body of one of their citizens, Jay Dickerson, owner of a small ranch, lying in the blood stained dirt. It was just after daylight when Simon Harper had found the body as he walked to open his general store and got everyone's attention to the murder.

"Has anyone gone to get the sheriff" Simon shouted, again anger showing in his tone.

"Billy Poole has," a man answered.

"Here comes Doc.," another man said. The crowd parted as Jess Bailey, the town doctor who also doubled as the town vet and undertaker made his way to where Dickerson lay.

"Who is it this time, Simon?" he asked as he looked at the man lying face down in an enormous pool of dried blood.

"Jay Dickerson," Simon said.

"The damn bastard cut his ears off," Simon said.

El Diablo

Doc looked at Simon and then at the body. "Ja…Jay Dickerson," he mumbled and dropped on a knee beside the body, picked up his friends arm and felt for a pulse.

"No sense in that Doc, he's deader than a piece of old wood," a man said standing behind Doc. Doc turned the body of his friend over and almost gagged as did some of the men. Jay's head flopped to one side, his throat cut so deep the head was barely attached to the body.

"Damn, another one," someone mumbled in the crowd referring to this murder as being like the other seven that had occurred in the last four months.

"Here comes Sheriff Teague," a man said looking at the man hurrying to where the crowd was.

The town of Santa Angelina was in a state of panic. In the last four months seven, now eight, of their citizens had been brutally murdered for no apparent reason. Sheriff Teague had not found one witness nor could he tie any of the victims together to come up with a reason.

After kneeling down and looking at the face of a man who had been his friend he slowly stood up and asked the question that he knew the answer before he asked it. "Anyone see anything?" Dead silence followed his question just like he figured.

"What are you going to do about this Sheriff?" Simon asked. "This is what, the eighth murder and you haven't made one arrest."

"I'm as frustrated as all of you are," Teague answered. "It's hard to make an arrest when not one person will come forward and say they saw anything and none of the victims were close friends or had any connections I can come up with."

"What the hell are we gonna do then Sheriff?" a man in the crowd asked. "It's not safe to go anywhere after dark no more."

"You got any damn leads on anyone Sheriff?"

Teague sensed the crowd's attitude was getting nasty over his not being able to solve the crimes. "We're going to stay calm. These murders are way over yours and my head. I've sent for help and I received a wire back from the U.S. Marshal's office in San Antonio. We should have a marshal or two here in a couple days, maybe sooner. They have experience in handling situations like this so maybe they can get to the bottom of these murders. We need to just stay calm and wait and see what they can do."

That afternoon, after two and a half days of steady riding Tye and Sam sat on a low rise overlooking the town of Santa Angelina and nearby Fort Concho.

"There she is Sam," Tye muttered then turned to his friend and fellow marshal. "You ready to earn our pay?"

"I need a damn bath," Sam, answered. "I smell worse than a stinking polecat."

"I noticed," Tye said laughing.

"Well pard, I ain't the only one. I noticed even Sandy turned his head when you walked by to saddle him." They both laughed and nudged their mounts down the hill toward the town. Several of the townspeople watched them as they rode in and each wondered who they were and each hoped they were the marshals that Sheriff Teague had requested. Tye and Sam noticed the stares from the people on the street as they reined in front of the building with the sheriff's sign above the door and dismounted. The door opened while they were tying their mounts reins to the hitching rail. A tall, lanky man with a badge on his chest stepped out.

"Something I can do for you men," he asked?

"You Sheriff Teague," Tye asked? The sheriff nodded.

Tye stepped on the porch and stuck out his hand. "I'm Marshal Tye Watkins and this man here," nodding to Sam who was stepping up on the porch, "Is Marshal Sam Jenkins." Sam shook the sheriff's hand.

"You the scout at Fort Clark?"

Seems every place he goes the same question comes up. Tye nodded and replied. "Was, but I'm a Deputy U.S. Marshall now."

Teague smiled. "Chasing bad guys instead of Apaches."

Tye smiled. "Yep, but found out it can be harder sometimes and a lot more dangerous than chasing Apaches."

"Well," Teague said smiling, "Let's go in and sit down, have a cup of coffee and palaver about why you are here." The three men walked into the office. Tye glanced around and quickly noted it was like all the other sheriff's office's he had been in; a desk with a chair behind it and two other chairs in front; a gun rack with a shotgun, two Henry rifles and a big Sharps fifty; a poster board with several wanted posters and a door that he figured led to the cells. The only exception was that this office was immaculate; no dust anywhere and everything in its place. He was impressed. He noticed Sam looking around also.

They sat down and the sheriff poured them each a cup of coffee. Teague already had one he had been drinking and as the sheriff sat down Tye spoke.

"Fill us in on what's happening Sheriff."

Teague took a sip and leaned back in his chair and shook his head and begin to talk. "Four months or so ago, we found a rancher by the name of Lester Cribs lying in the alley with his head damn near cut off. He had a small ranch east of here with his wife and teenage son. They hadn't much money and no enemies I could find, in fact, everyone liked Lester. No one I could find had seen or heard anything. He had been in the Double Ace Saloon having a couple drinks with a friend before heading home. No arguments with anyone." Teague took another sip of the strong coffee.

"The second killing was about a month later and the victim was a stranger that had just come into town. He rode in about an hour before the sun went down and was dead by eleven that night. His neck was cut like Lester's and no witnesses and no apparent reason." He then recounted each murder in detail finishing with the one just the night before.

When he finished, he leaned back in his chair, took a sip of coffee and said, "That's about it gents. No leads, no suspects, and a lot of anger toward this here ole boy sitting in this chair. I don't mind telling you I'm purely bamboozled and hopping mad over this situation, but I'm simply at the trails end and nowhere to go. That's why I sent for help."

Tye looked at Sam and then back at Sheriff Teague. "Let me ask you something Sheriff. Did a stranger come into town shortly before the first murder?"

Teague shook his head. "I know what trail you are heading down and I already checked on that angle. No one had come in that stayed that I could find."

"Alright," Tye said. "Have you thought of a soldier at the fort as being the killer?"

Teague nodded. "I checked with the Post Commander and no one was on leave on the nights of the murders."

"That pretty well means it's one of your citizens then," Sam said.

"Is the man who was killed last night still above ground," Tye asked?

"Yes he is," Teague answered. "The funeral is tomorrow afternoon. He's at docs."

"We're going to check into the hotel and wash some of the trail dust off and then we'd like to look at the body. Can that be arranged," Tye asked?

"I'll clear it with Doc Bailey. When you're ready, come by and I'll take you to him." Tye and Sam got up and went outside to their horses. Several townspeople were standing around.

"Those the marshal's you said was coming Sheriff?" a voice from the crowd asked as Tye and Sam led their horses across the street to the rail in front of the hotel ignoring the crowd. Both men took their Henry's and saddlebags with them when they entered the hotel and registered for a room. They glanced back outside through the window and saw Teague talking to the men.

"Yes, they are the marshals I said were coming." Teague told them. "Leave them alone unless they want to talk to you and let them do their job. The tall one is Tye Watkins, the scout from Fort Clark." A murmur went through the crowd as all of the men had heard stories about the scout.

"Can't be him. Hell, I figured he had to be eight foot tall," one man said bringing laughter from the rest.

Tye walked into his room and it was like he figured it would be; a single bed, an old vanity with a cracked mirror, a wash basin with a bar of soap, a towel, and a kerosene lamp. *At least it appears to be clean,* he thought to himself. He pitched his saddle bags in the corner after taking a clean shirt out. He removed his shirt and washed his face, arms and upper body. He dried off with the towel and put the clean shirt on. He pinned the marshal's badge on and put on a black vest. He locked his door and rapped on Sam's room which was next door.

Sam opened the door and Tye stepped in and quickly noticed the room was identical to his except the mirror wasn't cracked. "Great room."

"Well, it's clean anyway," Sam said smiling while buttoning up his clean shirt. When he had it tucked in his pants and his gun belt strapped on he said walking toward the door. "Let's go see the body."

They stopped at the sheriff's office and Teague led them to Doc Bailey's. After introductions the three lawmen followed the doctor through a door into a back room. Tye figured the doc to be in his mid fifties, a little over weight, and from the pinkness of his cheeks, probably enjoyed more than a drink or two.

Jay Dickerson lay on a table, arms folded across his chest. Tye and Sam stood next to the table on opposite sides looking down at the dead man. He appeared to be in his early to mid forties, stocky and looked to be use to hard work. Tye turned one of Dickerson's hands over and looked at the palm. He found what he expected: Jay Dickerson was a man used to working with his hands.

"Any other wounds on him Doc?" Tye questioned.

"Well, no, but to be honest with you I did not look for any others."

Tye nodded and knew why the doc hadn't looked. *I probably would not have either after seeing my friend killed like that and it being obvious as to how he died.* "You notice anything about the cut Sam?"

Sam bent over the body for a closer look then straightened up. "Throats cut so deep he was almost decapitated is all."

"All the victims cut identical Doc?" Tye asked looking across the table where Teague and the doc were standing.

"Yes," Doc Bailey answered. "The cuts all started just below the left ear, across the throat and ended up here" he said pointing to a place midway between the right ear and the larynx."Is that important?

"Stand in front of me Sam and pretend you have a knife in your hand and going to cut my throat." Sam walked around the table and stood in front of Tye. "Go ahead," Tye said. Sam's right hand came up and slashed down at Tye from right to left. "Now," Tye said pulling his 10" Bowie from the sheath in the top of his right boot and placing it against Sam's neck where the knife would have struck by Sam's swing. The tip was under Sams's right ear.

"I'll be damned," Doc said with a surprised expression on his face. "With the wounds on all the men starting under the left ear indicates the killer may be left handed."

Tye nodded. "Unless the killer struck from behind." A knock on the door prevented any more discussion. Doc opened the door and found a distraught Mrs. Dickerson and their teenage son standing there. Doc led her to his bed and sat her down on it. He took a glass and put a small shot of rot gut in it and had her drink it. She gagged and almost spit it out, but to her credit, she didn't. The burning liquor brought her out of her stupor and she looked around as if she just realized where she was.

"She has been that way since early this morning when Bill Maher come riding in from town with the news about pa," the young man said. "She was hysterical for awhile then sort of went into a sort of dazed state like she didn't know what was going on."

Doc nodded his head and turned back to Betty Dickerson. "You need another drink Betty?"

"Ju…just some water please." Sheriff Teague hurried over to the pump and returned with a glass of water which she drank about half before handing it back. "Thanks Sheriff Teague."

Doc took both of her hands in his. "I want you to know how sorry I and everyone in town are for your loss Betty. Jay was a good man and was well liked."

"Then why was he killed," she asked with tears again flowing down her cheeks.

Tye looked at her and thought to himself how Rebecca would react to his death. He thought of Little Ben and Nicole and what would happen to them. It brought a lump to his throat, but then he thought of Buff and the O'Malley's and knew that Rebecca and the kids would be taken care of. He felt much better with that thought. He thought again how tough these women had to be that come out here to this land with their man.

"We don't know that yet, Betty," Sheriff Teague said. He had taken his hat off. "Betty, these two men here," he said nodding to Tye and Sam, "are U.S. Marshalls and has been sent here to find the killer and end these senseless murders."

Tye had his hat in his hand and looked at the lady. "Sorry for your loss ma'am. My partner here," he nodded to Sam, "and me hope we can end these murders but we're going to need everyone's help to do it. This is probably not the right time, but could I ask you a few questions. We'd understand if you don't want to talk right now."

Betty nodded that she would and her and her son sat down at the table. They heard the pump handle working and Doc brought a glass of water. She drank deeply from the glass, sat it down and looked up at Tye waiting for the questions.

Tye felt uncomfortable and kept twisting his hat around in front of himself trying to figure out what to say to a lady who had just lost her husband and only means of support. Betty smiled at him. "Why don't you sit down Marshall so I don't have to look up to you?"

"Yes ma'am," Tye said laying his hat on the table and sitting down. "What was your husband doing in town last night?"

"He came in town to pay a note off at the bank. He had sold three horses and a few head of cattle and was going to settle up with the bank."

Tye nodded and then asked. "What was he doing in the saloon last night?"

Betty sobbed. "Every time he came to town he liked to visit with some of his friends and share a drink or two like most men do. He wasn't a gambler and never drank so much as to get drunk."

Sheriff Teague spoke up. "I never saw Jay have mor'n two or three drinks and not the hard stuff, only beer. Marvin Cates who works at the bank told me that Jay had been in and settled his debts."

Tye leaned toward Mrs. Dickerson. "Just one more question Ma'am. Did your husband have any enemies or disagreements with anyone that you know of?"

Betty shook her head. "No, not that I know of. Jay was a good man, worked hard, minded his own business and did his best to support us." She reached and took her son's hand in hers. "I really don't think he had an enemy in the world Marshal."

Tye nodded. "Sheriff Teague here told us that everyone liked Jay but sometimes we don't know everything about a person like his family does."

Betty nodded. "I understand that." She looked at the officers. "Anything else? If not, I would like to see my husband."

Sheriff Teague opened the door. "No more questions Betty and I want you to know again how sorry we are about your loss." Betty nodded as she walked out with her son and Doc. into the room where her husband lay.

"I see what you meant by no rhyme or reason for the killings," Tye said to Teague as the three men sat down.

El Diablo

"No one kills for no reason," Sam said. "There's something here, something that we are not seeing."

"There's always a chance of it being someone that's just crazy," Tye said.

"Ain't no one round here that's crazy I know of," Teague stated.

"Tye may be right, Sheriff. Three years ago we had a case similar to this when I was in Fort Worth. Someone was killing women, raping them and then brutally murdering them. When we caught him, it was a local man who everyone liked. He was as sane as me or you most of the time, but then little voices he said would tell him to do this or that. He was as crazy as a loon, but no one ever expected him of it."

"How did ya'll catch him?" Teague asked.

"He finally made a mistake after killing seven women. The last victim didn't die right away, lived long enough to describe her attacker and that she had stabbed him in the shoulder with a long hat pin. Her description fit several men, but she said she recognized him from one of the stores she shopped at. She died before she could name the store. We rounded up some men that worked at the local stores at that fit the description and had them take off their shirts. One had a wound in his shoulder. The town tried him and hung him and there were no more killings." Sam took a drink of coffee. "He was as normal as me or you ninety-nine per cent of the time, but the other one per cent was terrible. Even his wife didn't know about it."

"He was married?" an astonished Teague asked.

"Yep, and two kids."

"Damn," Teague muttered. "If it is someone like that how in hell do we flush him out?"

Tye sat his coffee cup down. "We don't know that's the case. We go ahead and ask our questions, look around, keep our eyes and ears open." He looked at Teague. "Not one word to anyone, not even your wife about it being a crazy-understood?" Teague nodded. "Go about your usual business sheriff, Sam and I will look around."

The two entered the nearest eating place to fill their bellies before starting their investigation. After ordering their food and drinking a cup of coffee Tye leaned back and thought about his family and what was going on back at Fort Clark. He enjoyed the marshaling job, but he found out he was gone longer and more often than he was when he was scouting for the army at Clark and that part he did not like. His two kids were growing fast and he wasn't around that much to watch. He knew the scouting was in good hands since the coming of the Black Seminole Indians to Clark a few months ago. But... he missed the tracking of the Apaches, the night camps with the soldiers, the hours of boredom on the trail and the moments of sheer terror of an Apache attack. He needed to think on things.

El Diablo

Chapter Two

Lieutenant John Bullis led his small patrol from Fort Clark along a narrow trail near Eagle's Nest near what is now Langtry, Texas. Bullis was with seven of his Black Seminole scouts and were trailing a band of Comanche that had raided a ranch killing two of the hands that worked there and stole several horses. Lt. Bullis had a distinguished career in the Civil War and as an Indian fighter after and now had been given the command of the Black Seminole Scouts at Fort Clark several months earlier. They, Bullis and the scouts, had so far held their own against the elusive enemy and were actually getting control of the Apache along the Border. The Comanche however, were another matter.

The scouts were black slaves that had escaped from brutal plantation owners' in the early 1800's, years before the Civil War. They found their way to Florida where they were adopted into the Seminole tribe by the war chief,

Osceola. They were good fighters and married into the tribe. Later, when the U.S. Army forced the Seminoles from Florida, most ended up on a reservation in Oklahoma. A large group escaped the reservation and settled in south Texas near what is now Eagle Pass on the Rio Grande River. Due to their fighting and tracking ability they were enlisted as scouts at Fort Clark.

It was noon when Bullis held up his hand to halt the troops. His scout, Pompey Factor, was approaching them.

"What did you find, Pompey?"

"Comanche Sir. Bout two mile ahead. Must be bout thirty or so." Factor replied. "Tha acting like they ain't in no hurry none. Guess they don't think anyone on their trail."

Bullis turned to his men. "Hear that men. Bout thirty or so. There's eight of us. Four to one odds are pretty good." The men nodded and laughed. They loved their leader and would ride into hell for him…which they might just do in a short time. "How about it-want to kill some Comanche?" His question was answered by some whoops and hollers. "Let's go get them then. Lead the way Pompey." He turned back with a smile to his men. "I know you are anxious, but keep it quiet. They started out at a trot and Bullis was thinking. *There's no backing down in any of these men. It's all forward and be damned the consequences.* He smiled. *That's why I respect them so much.*

El Diablo

Ten minutes later they halted as Pompey dismounted and signaled them to be quiet. He crawled up a hill and peered over the crest. The Comanche were still there, squatting by a fire and a spring. There were no guards he could see. The slope down wasn't so steep the men could not ride their horses down quickly and be on them in a few seconds. Of course he knew that in a few seconds the Redman could mount an attack or an effective escape. He scrambled back down the slope to Bullis and the other scouts.

"Da still thar Lt. We can leed our horses to near the top, mount and charge over da hill and surprise' um."

"How far from the top to the bottom?"

"Mabee fiftee yards."

"Okay men. Pistols only. Lead your mounts up the slope and then mount and charge over that damn hill like the devil is chasing you when I say so. Make a lot of noise as you do." He laughed. "Maybe we can scare them some." That brought some smiles to the men's faces. Yes suh, their Bullis was not afraid of nutin.

A tap on his shoulder brought Tye back to the present. "Looked like you were in someplace else partner." Sam said.

"Just reflecting back." Tye answered. "Wondering what's going on at home and at the fort."

"If I had a wife as pretty as yours I be damned if I'd go tramping off across the country looking to get myself maybe killed by some crazy outlaw."

Tye just smiled. This wasn't the first time Sam had mentioned that point. *Come to think of it, it doesn't make a lot of sense*, he thought. *The problem is I don't have a trade I could make a living at. Tracking and scouting is the only thing I know. When Ben gets a little older I'll teach him the things I know, but I'm gonna make dang sure someone teaches him a trade he can make a living with. Times are changing and one day the Indian problem will end and lawman will tame this country somewhat making it safer for decent folks. Till that day comes though men like me and Sam here will just do the best we can to rid this country of varmints.*

The soldiers came charging down the hill screaming and firing their pistols with Bullis in the lead. This was another reason the scouts loved him. As one would later say,"That thar Lootenent Bullis don't say go git'um men he leeds saying, "let's go get'um men." The Comanche were caught completely by surprise and many broke for their horses. The ones who didn't made an attempt to put up a defense but were quickly over run and shot. Some that were not shot were trampled by the soldier's horses. Bullis kept his horse headed toward the fleeing Comanche. After a mile he knew he wasn't going to catch them and raised his arm signaling a halt. They returned to the Comanche camp and made sure no warriors were still alive. Then they rounded up the stolen horses and some of the Indian ponies as well and started back toward Fort Clark.

"I thinks we gave them red devils the ole whut fur Suh," Sergeant Paine chuckled as he rode behind the lieutenant. Bullis turned in the saddle, looked at the sergeant who always wore a hat made from a buffalo skull complete with the horns and smiled. *God, I love these men,* he thought to himself again.

NOTE: The Seminole Scouts were runaway slaves that had escaped the plantation long before the Civil War and ended up in Florida. Being excellent fighters they were adopted into the Seminole tribe. When the U.S. Army forced the Seminole Indians to surrender most were sent to a reservation in Oklahoma. Not liking reservation life they escaped and settled on the Texas/Mexico Border near where Eagle Pass, Texas is now located in south Texas. The scout's graves are in Seminole Cemetery southwest of Fort Clark. Four of the scouts received The Medal of Honor and their graves have a white picket fence around them and an American Flag. They were Pvt. Pompey Factor, Sgt. John Ward, trumpeter Isaac Payne, and Private Adam Paine. You can visit the cemetery today.

Chapter Three

The man squatted by the fire poking the flames with a stick and watching the sparks rise into the air to be carried off by the slight southwest breeze. The sun was almost down and darkness would soon surround him. He wasn't a big man, five foot nine and lean, but surprising strength lay hidden under the dark brown skin. Coal black hair fell loosely to his shoulders. A red bandana wrapped around his forehead, a white streak across his nose and cheeks and a deerskin vest covered his upper torso. Leather leggings covered his legs and were tucked into knee high moccasins. A breechcloth hung around his waist over his leggings. If one met him he looked like an Apache till you looked into his eyes which were steel gray. Lately, any man that had looked into those eyes was the last thing they saw.

Jeb Summers was twenty three years old. His father was white and his mother had been a full blood Jicarilla Apache. Being a breed he was never accepted in the white man's world and had no friends except the boys in his mother's Apache band and he never felt really accepted by them either. His life had ended twelve years ago when some men came to his parent's home, killed his father and after raping his mother, slit her throat. Jed was away hunting when this happened and arrived just in time to see the men ride off. He was devastated and after burying his parents made his way to his mother's band and lived with her sister and her husband until recently. During that time he became a proven warrior and hunter.

He had killed four Comanche warriors one summer day when he was seventeen that had attacked his band. He had killed two white men, a trapper and a buffalo hunter. He had gained great status as a warrior with his people, but were they his people? A man whose blood is neither white nor red; a breed truly feels that he belongs nowhere. At twenty summers of age his life changed again when a band of Mexican soldiers charged into their small camp at daybreak and killing everyone except him and a young girl of seven. His wife and child were among the ones killed. The wounded girl later died in his arms. He swore revenge and the next day started his killing rampage. What had started out as a trail of vengeance had since turned into something dark and evil; he was now getting self gratification from killing, something akin to a sexual act with a woman. He lay down remembering the first of his kills.

The adobe house sat at the base of a hill with smoke curling out of the chimney and drifting off with the early morning breeze. Jeb lay on his stomach behind a salt cedar about thirty yards away watching. A tall, thin Mexican man came out and walked to a small building west of the house. He opened the door walked in and closed it. Jeb rushed the house and crashed through the door surprising a woman who was getting dressed. Her scream was cut short by a blade across her throat. She made a gurgling sound as she fell to the floor as her life blood pumped from the wound.

Jeb turned as the man came rushing in and seeing the Apache he rushed to his right toward the wall where his rifle was hanging. Jeb was quicker and caught him from behind and pulling his head back with his left hand and slashed the man's throat to the bone with his Bowie in his right. He released his hold on the man's head and he fell to the floor. His legs jerked a few times and then were still. Looking quickly around he spotted a small boy of maybe eight sitting up in bed.

Jeb walked to the youngster and sat down on the bed. He spoke to the boy in Spanish. "When someone comes tell them El Diablo was here and they will see more of him. Understand?" The boy nodded his head and as Jeb walked away he heard the boy sobbing softly as he had done when his parents were killed so many year ago.

The killing of the man and woman was only the beginning. He had lost count of how many he had killed. The very name of El Diablo brought fear into every Mexican that lived along the Border of Texas and Mexico. Every man slept with a gun by his bed, doors and window shutters locked even on the hottest nights. Better to be a little uncomfortable than dead was the general feeling. The

El Diablo

Federales put a reward out on him, dead or alive which resulted in lots of Apaches being shot on sight.

Jeb never killed a child and these boys and girls were brought into to look at the dead Apache bodies being brought in hoping to identify one as El Diablo. None were so far.

The heat was on him from the Federal troops, trappers, hunters, and every male in the region. He decided to cross the Rio Bravo River (Rio Grande), into Texas and kill some white eyes. He made his way north east bypassing the fort called Fort Davis and found the town of San Angelina (later named San Angelo).

He killed his first man in the alley beside the drinking place called the Double Ace Saloon. He killed four more in that same place, one outside of the man's home and two more in other places in town.

Each of the killings was becoming more brutal; ears and noses being cut off, multiple stab wounds. The town was up in arms now and alert for any sign of trouble. El Diablo took special satisfaction from killing now right under the lawmen and soldiers noses. The white eyes are as stupid as the Mexicans, he thought. The last killing two nights ago was again in the alley where he had killed others bringing even more satisfaction to him. The killing now was as satisfying as being with a woman. The wait and stalking his victim was like foreplay, and the actual killing brought a release of pure ecstasy from him-pure gratification.

He continued to stroke the fire and finally, with full dark around him and the fire now only burning coals he lay on his blankets and was soon fast asleep.

"I dunno about this one," Sam mumbled more to himself than anyone else while sitting with Teague and Tye.

"What did you say?" Tye asked.

Sam looked at him and shook his head. "Nothing, just thinking out loud." He looked away and said. "If I didn't know better I'd say El Diablo has come to Texas."

Sheriff looked at Sam and then at Tye. "What in hell's name is he talking about? Who is this El Diablo?

"A breed, Sheriff. A breed on a vengeance trail like you would not believe." Sam answered. "No telling how many he has killed in Mexico and he kills by cutting people's throats and then hacking them up."

"And you think this El Diablo could be here?

"I don't know sheriff. As far as I know he's never been caught and with all the heat that's been on him he might have lit a shuck for Texas." The three men were quite for a moment each lost in his thoughts about what might be. "It's late," Tye said. "Let's get some shut eye."

It was about midnight when the breed mounted his horse and rode to the town of San Angelina. He left his horse about a hundred yards in the mesquite behind the livery stable and made his way to the back of the barn. He waited a full five minutes making sure no one was in the shadows' before he moved to the side of the livery and worked his way slowly to the corner by the walkway. He crouched in the shadows and waited patiently, as only an Apache could. Thirty minutes later he heard footsteps and his pulse quickened. He slipped his razor sharp knife from the sheath and slowly stood up, remaining invisible in the shadows. His pulse quickened and sweat broke out on his forehead.

As the man walked by he stepped out behind him and grabbed his forehead with his left hand and jerked the man's head back exposing his throat which he quickly slashed with the Bowie. The blade cut deep and blood spurt several feet. He released his hold and the man fell to the wooden walkway. He fell on his side where his pistol hung and the handle made a pretty loud noise as it struck the wooden planks. A man shouted from across the street and the glow of a lamp shone through the window of the livery as a lamp was turned up. El Diablo ran quickly back the way he had come and for a brief second or so he was in the light from the livery. The man who had yelled fired his Colt, but hit nothing.

The blast from the Colt brought the lawmen to their feet and out the door. Men were shouting in front of the livery so the three lawmen ran there with their Colts drawn.

Arriving Teague grabbed the first man he came to. It was Simon Caldwell the owner of the livery. "What's going on Simon," Teague asked?

'I heard a noise outside my window and then a shot. I ran outside and saw Bill running from across the street and a man lying on the walkway."

"Did you see anything else," Tye asked.

"No, but you might ask Bill over there." Tye and Sam walked over to Bill while Teague knelt beside the man lying on the walk.

"Tell me what you saw," Tye said as he stood in front of the man named Bill.

"Only got a glimpse when he ran through the light from the window there," he said nodding to the window on the side of the livery."I swear unless my eyes were paying tricks on me, it was a damn Apache. I shot at him, but I missed. Never was no account with a pistol."

Tye looked at Sam who was looking back. They both knew hell was here; El Diablo had come calling to San Angelina.

"You two shor have funny looks on your faces," Teague said walking up to the two lawmen. "You find out anything?"

"Yeah, we did," Sam replied, "And you ain't gonna like it one damn bit."

"Who's the man laying over there?" Tye asked.

Teague looked over his shoulder at the man. "Dunno. I haven't seen him before. He must have ridden in after dark." Doc Bailey arrived at that time to take care of the body. Teague looked at Bill. "Bill, get someone to help you and take the body to Doc's." Bill nodded.

"Let's go to your office Teague and talk," Tye suggested. Once there, Teague turned up the lamp and lit the stove to heat up some coffee.

"What did Bill tell you that had you two looking like you had seen a ghost or something?"

They sat down at the desk. Sam spoke. "Bill said he only got a glimpse of the man as he ran through the light from the window of the livery. He said he thought it was an Apache."

"An Apache!" Teague said astonished. "Hell, we haven't had any trouble with them devils in a long time."

"This may be no ordinary Apache Sheriff," Sam said. Teague looked at Sam and then at Tye.

"Would you two just spit it out and let me in on what you are thinking?"Then asked. "Wait just a damn minute. You're not thinking..." He paused then added. "You're not thinking what I think you are thinking are you- El Diablo?"

Sam spoke up. "Last we heard he had not been captured or killed. Like we talked about earlier, with the Federal troops, the law and every Mexican along the Border looking for him Mexico may have gotten a little warm for him."

"So you think maybe he's come across the Border to kill white folks for a change?" Teague said standing up and walking to the window.

"Can't say for sure sheriff but the facts are out there. El Diablo kills with a knife by cutting people's throats. He moves like a ghost and till tonight was seldom seen except by his victims or by children. As far as we know he's still running loose."

Teague looked down at the two men sitting around the desk. "Why children?"

Sam answered. "For some unknown reason he kills men and women and thinks no more of it than you or me killing a fly, but he never harms a child."

"And you two think he is here…in San Angelina?"

"I'd bet on it, Sheriff," Tye said. "Sam and I will get on his tracks at first light."

"I think you had better have a meeting with the town council and tell them. I wouldn't mention the name of El Diablo though because that might scare people more than they are," Sam said.

"What do I tell them then?"

"Tell them the killer left tracks this time and the best damn tracker in Texas is on his trail," Sam said nodding toward Tye. "We'll get him."

El Diablo

"El Diablo…here…in my town," Teague sat down hard in his chair…"Damn!"

Chapter Four

Dawn found Tye and Sam leading their horses away from the livery following the footprints of the killer. Sheriff Teague had roused the owner of the hardware store early so they could get supplies for a week. A pack horse followed Sam's mount a halter rope tied to the horn on Sams' saddle. They found where the killer's horse had been picketed. Tye picked up the horses tracks quickly. They mounted and begin following them.

"Keep your eyes peeled for any movement or sign of trouble Sam while I keep mine on the tracks," Tye said. "He's a smart one. He's using the rocks to hide his tracks." Tye dismounted several times in the next hour studying the ground. Sam could see nothing but packed dirt and rocks and once more was amazed at Tye's ability to read sign and follow unseen tracks by him. Suddenly Tye pulled up. He turned to Sam and whispered.

"Dismount and be quiet. Take the horses over there and picket them." He nodded to a stand of large cedars.

When the horses had been picketed Sam eased quietly up to him.

"What is it?" He whispered..

"Take a whiff of the air and tell me what you smell."

Sam turned his head up toward the sky and sniffed. "Smoke-a campfire." Tye nodded and motioned for him to follow him after putting his finger to his lips indicating Sam needed to be damn quiet. Ten minutes later they were standing by the still warm coals of the small fire. Looking around Tye said.

"He's been here for awhile. I'd say a month or more if I was guessing"

"How you figure that?"

"Ain't hard if a man will study on things. For one, that fire has had many fires in it from looking at the amount of coals." He nodded toward where the man's horse had been picketed. "Look at the droppings. Enough there for a small herd. More than one night's pile of coffee grounds over there also and look at all the bones of rabbit, squirrels and birds scattered around. Yeah, I'd say he's called this place home for awhile." Tye walked over to where the horse had been picketed and studied the area while Sam stood amazed at what this man could see and figure out.

Tye came back. "He stopped here long enough to gather his things and lit out headed east. I guess he knew things were over here when that man Bill saw him and took a shot. Figured he'd be tracked here so he lit out to greener pastures. Left about four hours ago headed east."

"Well now Mr. Tracker do you also know where he's going?" Sam asked pushing the brim of his hat up and smiling.

"Nope, but I can guess why."

"Why east then?"

"People. There's a lot more people east than west."

"A lot more to kill," Sam muttered nodding his understanding.

"Well, there are forts to the north and south and that area will be pretty well patrolled. West is Mexico and its pretty hot for him over there. East is pretty open, not too many towns but there are probably a lot of ranchers and farmers for the bastard to prey on."

"Why is what I keep asking myself? Why all the killing?"

"He's El Diablo and he's not afraid of anyone or anything. I really think he doesn't care if he lives or dies. He has a hate for some reason of all men and he's going to kill till he's killed. Maybe we will know someday why. I will tell you this; I don't think he will be one that will be taken alive, and anyone that tries is asking for his throat to be slit. This is one hombre that scares me some."

Sam laughed at the last statement. "Hell Tye, you aren't afraid of anything not even the devil himself."

"Only a fool or a crazy man is never scared Sam. I'm was scared plenty times when fighting Apaches and even a couple times since chasing outlaws. Being scared is normal it's just the way you handle it that separates men. I've seen plenty of men who were scared, but were able to function and do their job. Then I've seen men, good men, fall to pieces. I've seen you scared Sam, but you are one that can handle it well. My pa would say you are a man to ride the river with and that's about the best you can say for a man out here."

Sam cleared his throat. "Let's ride then and get this son-of-a-bitch before he kills anyone else. Sam rode a little taller in the saddle as he thought about what Tye said about him. *That's something coming from him. The fact that he's scared sometimes makes me feel better too.*

Jeb, El Diablo, rode easy across the prairie southeast of San Angela where the landscape was mostly flat with only an occasional hill here and there. There didn't appear to be much of anything taller than a man's head. A few mesquites, salt cedars, cactus and grass were all a man could see. No sign of wildlife other than a buzzard or two and no sign of water. He had been riding for hours when suddenly he reined his mount to a halt. Wagon tracks and not very old headed on a southern trail. He dismounted and looking at the horses tracks looked south, the direction the wagon was headed. He remounted and then stood on his horses back so he could see farther. He saw the white canopy of the wagon about two miles from where he was. He smiled and slipped down on his mounts back and headed south.

Bill Whitson, his wife Betty, and their eight year old twins, Billy and Elizabeth had come down from Kansas hoping to end up around Brackett where they had heard land was for the taking. They had been traveling for two months and were happy their trek south was only a few days from ending. They had made it through the Indian Territory in what later would be Oklahoma safely with the many wagons that made up their train from Kansas. Only three wagons accompanied them when they left Fort Worth and those three stayed and settled around Fort Griffin when they arrived there. The Whitson's continued south toward Fort Mckavett alone skirting the area known as the Staked Plains where the Comanche Quanah Parker was raiding. They would rest a couple days at Fort Mckavett and restock their supplies. From there they would head southwest to Brackett. Good times were only a couple weeks away they figured. They figured wrong.

While resting and eating their noon meal they did not know they were being watched. Jeb had moved within seventy-five yards of their wagon from the downwind side not taking any chances of the horses seeing or smelling his horses. He watched the kids playing and it reminded him of the young boys and girls that played in his camp what seemed years ago before they were killed by raiding Mexicans for the bounty being paid by the Mexican government for Apache scalps. The slight smile that was beginning to form on his lip as he watched faded quickly at that thought.

The man had a Colt on his hip and when he stood up he reached down and picked up his Henry repeater. *Cautious man*, Jed thought as he eased his own Henry to his shoulder and fixed the front sight in the center of the man's chest. He touched the trigger slightly and then slowly squeezed. The Henry bucked against his shoulder and flame belched from the barrel as it spit its deadly load toward its target.

Tye knelt with one knee on the ground studying the tracks; wagon tracks and the horses they had been following. He stood up slowly.

"What is it Tye?"

"He came across these wagon tracks about two maybe three hours ago. He's following them."

"How old are the wagon tracks?"

"Not much older than his. He's gonna kill them and there ain't a damn thing we can do about it." He mounted Sandy. "Let's ride," and took off at a gallop. He knew there was no sense wasting time looking for horse tracks since the wagon tracks were plain enough.

The .44 Caliber slug from Jeb's rifle caught Bill Whitson in the chest and exploded his heart before exiting out the back. Almost before the sound of the first shot had ended Jed swung the barrel to the right slightly and fired again. The second round caught Betty in the side of the head as she screamed for her husband who was falling to the ground. The two children sat frozen, unable to move for a couple seconds then Elizabeth screamed and ran to her mother. Billy ran to his father. Both mother and father were dead. Billy heard a noise and turned to see an Indian walking into the camp holding a rifle. He picked up a rock and threw it at the man who dodged it easily and kept coming. He ran to his sister and together they ran into the brush to try and hide.

Jeb did not follow. He kicked the man in the side to make sure he was dead. He didn't bother with the woman; half her head was blown away. He got no gratification killing with a bullet; a knife was so much better, but they were dead and he was content with that. He took some of their supplies leaving enough for the kids to get by on for a few days. He left the man's pistol taking the rifle and a box of .44's. He walked back to where he left his horse, mounted and rode toward the east.

Tye and Sam rode into the camp about forty-five minutes later after riding and pushing their mounts hard.

El Diablo

They reined up suddenly when they saw a young boy pointing the old Navy Colt at them.

"Easy son," Tye said. "We're friendly. I'm Deputy Tye Watkins and this here ugly galoot is Deputy Marshal Sam Jenkins. We are following a bad man…" he paused as he started to ask if they had seen anyone when he noticed the two forms lying under the wagon with blankets on them. *God, not these kids folks,* he thought. Sam saw the blankets at the same time and vile tasting bile rose in his throat.

"Please put the gun down son. We're here to help not hurt you." He pointed to the star on his chest. He saw the boys eyes move from his to his chest and the gun lowered.

"We're going to dismount so you take it easy son," Tye said smiling.

Tye knelt on the ground in front of the two children and saw the anguish in their faces. They were scared too. *Hell, I would be too if I was left alone in the middle of nowhere and as young as these two.* "What happened here son?"

"My pa was standing up after eating our noon meal when he was shot," he answered and then broke into tears and said, " T…Th…then my ma was s..shot a second later,"he managed to say. The two children hugged each both crying. Sam turned his face away cursing the bastard half breed under his breath. Tye put his hand on the boys shoulder.

"What else son? Did you see the man who did this?"

"Yes, sir," he said trying to hold back more tears. He walked into camp and I threw a rock at him and then grabbed my sister's arm and ran to the bushes and hid."

"What happened then?" Sam asked.

"Dunno sir. We hid and after a few minutes we heard a horse trotting off. He took my pa's rifle and maybe a little food and a box of shells is all that I think are missing."

"What did this feller look like?" Tye asked.

"Didn't look close but it was an Indian."

"You have any relatives around here?" Sam asked kneeling in front of the children.

"No sir. We came from Kansas. We were going to a place called Brackett to get some land."

"That's where we are from," Tye said smiling.

"Really," the boy said trying hard to smile but only succeeded in his lips quivering some.

"Really," Sam said. "Tye lives there with his wife and two kids and a grumpy old man who used to be a real mountain man. Me, I'm a bachelor. Ain't found a woman who would have me yet. Well, that's not exactly true," he added. "There's a young lady who helped nurse me back to health after I was shot that I'm pretty fond of. Going back to see her as soon as we catch this polecat that shot your parents."

"A mountain man! One who trapped beaver that we read about in school?"

"A real mountain man son," Tye answered. "He trapped with my pa thirty-five plus years ago in the Rockies. He came to live with me and my family about four years ago and he can tell you a lot of stories about the mountains, grizzly bears, snow and ice, and Blackfoot, Ute and Shoshoni Indians."

The two men walked off a ways to talk. "What are we going to do now?" Sam asked. "We just can't leave the kids out here by their own selves all alone."

"I know that and I've been studying on it some." Tye rolled a smoke and struck a match and lit it. "Can you drive a wagon Sam?"

"Sure I can. What does that…wait a minute? You ain't thinking what I think you are thinking are you?"

"There's a lot of homesteads south of here. I was thinking you could drive the wagon to one of them, explain the situation and maybe they would take them in till we can get back by."

"While you track that damn breed by yourself?"

"Yeah, unless you think you can."

"You know better than that, but I don't like leaving you by yourself on that mans trail."

"As soon as you find a place for the kids ride back here. I'll leave a trail even you can follow," Tye said smiling.

Sam thought about it for a moment. "Okay. But make sure you mark it so I can find you. I hate leaving a man out here that is helpless as you are all by himself," he said laughing and reaching over to shake Tye's hand.

"It's settled then," Tye said. We'll see to the burying and then explain to the kids what the plan is."

An hour and a half later Tye sat on Sandy and watched the wagon pulling away. He had struggled to speak a few words over the kid's parents.

"Lord, I didn' know these folks but I believe they were good people. We found a family Bible and the kids said they read to them every night. Take them to your bosom Lord and when you see their folks up there tell them the kids are fine and going to be cared for. Lead Sam Lord in finding a good place for them to stay till we can come for them. Amen."

It was tough on the kids burying them and he knew they were probably in for a rough time for awhile. He knew Sam was a better talker than him so he hoped he could make them feel somewhat better about things. He reined Sandy east and picked up the breeds trail. He knew it was going to be a dangerous trail…just how tough and dangerous he could not imagine.

Chapter Five

Two hours after parting with Tye Sam pulled the wagon up on a knoll overlooking a ranch house complete with stable, corral, and a barn. A man stood in front of the house looking up at where Sam sat on the wagon seat. Sam snapped the reins and the team moved down the slope toward the house. He saw a woman come out and hand the man a rifle and she held one too.

The closer he got the more impressed he was with the place. The corral was built strong and had a watering trough along one side that was made of rock. The barn was well built and painted as was the house. Flowers were growing along the front of the house and along both sides of the long porch. These people were here to stay and from the look of them holding the rifles were as tough as nails. A mongrel dog was standing beside them yapping away.

Sam halted the wagon about thirty feet from the two and held up his hands.

"We're friendly," he said.

"Go ahead and step down then," the man said. Sam figured he had sized him up and with two kids beside him wasn't likely to cause no trouble.

Billy jumped down and Sam helped Elizabeth to the ground. "Obliged," Sam said. He turned to face the man and woman and saw the man's eyes go to his badge.

"You a lawman?"

"Yes sir," Sam answered quickly. "My name is Sam Jenkins and I'd like to talk to you and the Missus if you would let me."

The man reached out and shook hands with Sam. "Names Will Matlock and this here little lady is my wife of ten years, Millie. Sam tipped his hat to Millie.

"This here young man is Billy Whitson and this pretty little thing here is Elizabeth Whitson.

The lady spoke up. "Well don't just stand there palavering" She took the children's hands and started toward the house. "I just made some fresh apple pie that I think you two will love." Inside the house was just as Sam figured; neat and clean and even had a wooden floor. He took off his hat and sat at the table when the woman motioned for him to do so.

"Ma'am," Sam asked after sitting down. "Is that pie just for the kids?"

The lady laughed loud and hard. "No, there's enough for you too." Sam' face broke with a huge smile.

"Bet you two didn't expect this treat did you?' he said looking at Billy and Elizabeth who smiled for the first time since he and Tye found them.

"So, what are you doing out in this part of the country with two young kids?" Will asked.

Sam waited to answer trying to swallow a bite of the best damn apple pie he had ever tasted. "Pie's awful good Ma'am." He looked at Will. "Here's the way things lie Mr. Matlock. My partner, Tye Watkins and me were trailing this breed who has killed several people when we came across this wagon that belonged to these kids parents. The breed had killed both of them and left the kids to fend for themselves. We ta...." He was interrupted.

"This here Watkins the one who's the scout at Fort Clark?"

Sam nodded and thought, I *think every damn person in the whole State knows of him.* "Yes Sir, you've got the rascal pegged."

"Lots of stories about him. They true?"

Sam laughed. "I don't know which ones you have heard, but from what I've seen riding with him the last two or so years they probably are." The man nodded and seemed satisfied.

He looked at the kids then back at Sam. "They saw?"

Sam nodded. "Right before their eyes." Millie put her hand to her mouth.

"My God…how awful," she said and hugged them.

"Anyway, like I was saying. We were hoping I could find someone to watch over the children and then rejoin Tye who's trailing the breed. After we catch him then we can pick the children up and go back to Fort Clark and maybe find a home for them since their nearest kin is way up in Kansas."

Millie looked at her husband who nodded. "You just go ahead Sam. Me and my man will take good care of those two youngsters and be proud to do it."

"Obliged Ma'am. Much obliged," Sam said standing up. He walked around the table to where Billy and Elizabeth sat. He knelt down between them and whispered.

"Just as soon as Tye and me catch the man who killed your folks we will be back to get you. Okay?" He patted both on the shoulders. "Mind your manners while I'm gone." He stood up and started toward the door, a lump in his throat.

"Sam. Wait!" Elizabeth hollered. She was out of the chair and running to him. He knelt and she threw her arms around his neck. "You will come back won't you? Promise me you will. Promise."

Sam could hardly get the words out. He looked at Millie for help, but she had tears in her eyes and her hand on Billy's shoulder. "I…I promise," he managed to choke out. "I'll be back." He hugged her and then stood up and walked out the door not looking back so they would not see the tears in his eyes. He walked to his horse tied behind the wagon and stepped in the saddle. Will was standing there.

"Kids are wonderful Sam. They lost their parents a few hours ago and here they are now looking at you, depending on you."

Sam looked away not wanting to look the man in the eye and nodded.

Will put his hand on Sam's leg. "Ain't no shame in letting your feeling show Sam. I'd be the same way if I was in your boots. You find that bastard and get back here to these kids."

Sam looked down at the man and reached out and shook his hand and held it for a moment. "We don't know where this son-of-a-bitch is heading Will. But until we find him don't go anywhere without your gun and don't trust any stranger. I can't tell you what he looks like except he is half Apache and dresses like one, but that don't mean he can't change clothes. Just be careful and take care of your missus and those two kids." Will nodded and watched as Sam rode off.

Tye sat on a rock chewing some jerky and letting Sandy take a breather. He was impressed with this man he was trailing. The breed was traveling at a good clip but leaving little trail to follow. Every chance he got he walked his horse in a creek or found some rocky ground and Tye had to spend precious time figuring out the trail. This, plus leaving a trail himself for Sam to follow, had gotten him another hour or so behind the man. He figured he was at least three hours behind now, but at least he had been able to stay on the trail.

Jeb sat on his pony and looked at this back trail. He had that feeling he was being followed, but in the half dozen times he had stopped and watched had seen no one. He threw his right leg over the pony's back and slid to the ground and squatted, watching. He could see maybe three miles from where he sat on the bushy knoll and decided to watch for awhile. He reached into his pouch and took out some jerky and a biscuit he had taken from the wagon and slowly ate as he watched. After thirty minutes he decided no one was following and he stood and jumped easily onto his pony's back. He started to nudge the pony into a trot when he looked back and saw movement on the trail behind him. He turned and stared at the object and then remembered the looking glass he carried. He reached into his saddle bag and lifted the glass to his eyes shading the lens with his free hand so there would no flash of sunlight that could be seen for miles.

It was a man and he was riding a magnificent looking horse. As he watched the man stopped, dismounted and knelt down as if looking at tracks. That was enough to convince Jeb that the man was tracking him. *This is no ordinary white man, he thought. I have left little trail to follow. But now I know he comes, El Diablo will have* some *surprises for him.* He laughed. *They only send one man to find me...to kill me. That they do not know who they are dealing with will be clear to them soon. I will kill this man and cut off his head and leave it in front of the sheriff's door of the next town I come to.* He spit on the ground. "Stupid gringos" he said, and spit again in disgust.

Tye had seen the movement from a far distance as he mounted Sandy. He leaned forward and patted Sandy on the neck. "If that was him boy, he knows we are back here so I figure he will try to have a little surprise for me." He decided to close the gap some and put Sandy into a gallop to get to where he saw the man and horse and then he would slow down and study on things some.

Reaching the spot where he had seen the man Tye dismounted and looked around carefully. After a couple minutes he had things figured out. He was here for awhile, he thought. Stopped to watch his back trail and as long as he was here watching I figure he had a feeling he was being trailed. He stood and studied the terrain in the direction the tracks led. The land was mostly rolling hills with lots of cedar and occasional stands of mesquite and cactus. The grass was sparse as the land was rocky except in the bottom of draws where runoffs had cut deep into the land. There, in the sandy bottom of the draws, good grass could be found but not in abundance. The land was a little too rocky for farming and not enough good grass to run cattle unless a man had a hell of lot of it. It was however a good place to get one's self killed. The cedar and the arroyos that cut through the land offered plenty of good ambush sites.

Tye mounted Sandy and patted him on the neck. "Keep a sharp eye old friend. We are headed into trouble." He shucked his Henry from its leather and nudged Sandy with his heels. Sandy started down the low hill with Tye keeping one eye on the ground and the other for any sign of trouble. He also watched Sandy's ears for many a time Tye's life had been spared the possibility of being shot or hit by an arrow by Sandy's alerting him to trouble. For what seemed the ten thousandth time the last ten or twelve years his father's words came back to him when he was in situations like this. "Watch your horse as much as the trail because your horse will see or hear things before you do a lot of the time."

A quarter mile ahead of him Jeb lay behind a thick stand of cedar, the butt of the Henry nestled comfortably against his shoulder and waited. A slight smile formed on his lips in anticipation of another kill. He could not believe one gringo would have the nerve to chase him; or be so stupid.

He could see the rider now only two hundred or so yards off coming toward him as straight as a bee to water. He cocked the hammer on the Henry and waited not moving even as the gnats and flies hovered around him some landing on his hands and face. The rider was now a little over a hundred yards and disappeared behind some cedars. Jeb would shoot him as he appeared on this side and he moved the barrel slightly to the right exactly where the rider would appear. He saw the horse's head appear and began squeezing the trigger when he suddenly took his finger off the trigger; his eyes open wide in disbelief. The horse's saddle was empty. He quickly searched the area with his eyes without moving even his head.

Suddenly, a bullet cut the air only inches from his ear. He rolled to one side and got to his feet and ran in a crouch zigzagging toward his horse. He jerked the picket loose and leaping onto the back of the animal was running full speed in two seconds. Another bullet cut a crease across his arm just above the elbow. Nothing serious but it burned like fire.

He ran his mount about a mile and then slowed down to a trot and then a walk. He was visibly shaken. Never had a white man out foxed him and never had a white man drawn his blood. He would have to be a little more careful, a little more devious with this one. Whoever he was had Apache blood in him he bet.

Tye had not seen the man, but years tracking Apaches made him leery of the spot as he approached the stand of cedars. If he had been in Jeb's place and looking to ambush a man that would be the perfect spot. He slid from the saddle as Sandy walked behind the cedars and he worked his way on his belly to where he could see the cedars on the hill. He saw the rifle barrel protruding from the limbs, but not the man. He pointed the barrel of his Henry about thirty or so inches from the end of the barrel of Jeb's rifle and squeezed off a blind shot hoping he would get lucky. As soon as he fired he was up and running up the slope and dropped behind a large rock.

He heard the sound of a man running and was immediately up himself and running also. When he topped the crest of the hill he was out of breath, but saw the man riding away on his pony. He took a quick shot, but with his breathing hard and a moving target he knew he missed. Another look and he saw the man's left arm hanging straight down so he figured maybe he had winged him.

"Damn," he cursed and headed back down the slope to where Sandy stood. He quickly mounted and was up the slope in a few seconds and had Sandy in a gallop chasing the killer, the man known as El Diablo. *Well*, he thought, *he knows I'm after him now for sure. You can bet he will be a little more careful from now on. He's gonna be more dangerous than ever now that's for damn sure.* "I'll tell you one thing old partner, things are going to get real interesting from here on," he said to Sandy who nickered and shook his head. "Yes sir, real interesting."

Chapter Six

The Seminole Scouts led by Lieutenant Bullis rode into Fort Clark with the stolen horses. Sergeant Payne took Bullis' horse to the stables while the lieutenant made his report to the Post Commander, Major Thurston. After being announced he entered the office, saluted the major and received Thurston's thanks for a job well done. He walked over to the wall map and placed his finger where they had the encounter with the Comanche.

"I don't understand why the Comanche are raiding this far south, Sir. We've had no trouble that we know of for a long time. Besides, McKenzie had them pretty well whipped months ago after the Palo Duro Canyon battle where he killed all their horses and destroyed their food supply."

Thurston motioned for him to sit down which Bullis did so. "A lot of the Indians, Kiowa, Comanche, and Cheyenne as well as their leaders, Poor Buffalo and Lone

Wolf escaped with some horses. It's my guess they are trying to reestablish their horse herd any way they can. Army horses or horses from ranches are fair game to them as long as they feel the odds are on their side." He smiled. "They didn't figure on you and the Seminole Scouts though."

He continued. "You know Lieutenant, when our Chief of Scouts Tye Watkins left to become a U.S. Marshal, I was afraid things out here would go to hell in a hurry. I'm glad to say they haven't, thanks to you and the scouts."

"Thank you Sir. I'm really proud of them. I would put them up against any outfit in the whole damn army any time," Bullis replied. He took a cigar that Thurston offered, bit off the end and lit it. He inhaled deeply and looked at Thurston.

"Tell me about Watkins. I've heard some stories from some of the sergeants and even Captain McClellan that are pretty far out."

"Whatever you heard is probably true, Lieutenant."

"Really!"

Thurston nodded. "He's a remarkable man. He pretty much ended most of the Apache problem himself by killing several Apache warrior leaders in hand to hand fights. He brought in the vicious Vasquez gang. He tracked down Yancey Cates, the most vicious man I have ever seen or heard of in my whole life. He ended the Apache

Yahzie's reign of terror and they are now good friends. Believe this or not, but it's true. Awhile back, troops led by McClellan combined with the Apaches led by Yahzie and defeated a large force of Comanche led by none other than Quanah Parker himself and sent them high tailing back to north Texas. "

"They fought side by side!"

Thurston nodded and chuckled. "I couldn't believe it when I got McClellan's report, but it was true. Another thing about Tye, only one patrol that Tye scouted for was ever ambushed and it was because the officer didn't listen to him. The officer did after that and he is now one of my best."

"McClellan?"

Thurston nodded. "He was arrogant like a lot of young officers are. You know the type I'm talking about.'

Bullis nodded. "Thought he was above everyone else?"

Thurston nodded. "That ambush almost got him and all his men killed and would have if Tye hadn't pulled them out. He was a changed man after that and over a period of time the men grew to trust his judgment and had a lot of respect for him. Another time Tye ran almost forty miles on foot in the dark to the fort and then led a patrol back to rescue some troops pinned down by the Apaches. If I live to be a hundred, I'll never see a man his equal at fighting, tracking, and reading sign."

"I'd like to meet him someday."

"You will. He'll be back in here in a few days as soon as whoever he's chasing is caught or killed."

"You think a lot of him, Sir."

Thurston chuckled. "I'll tell you this Lieutenant. You would never want that man as an enemy or have him on your trail." He stood up and Bullis followed suit. "I know you must be tired so get cleaned up and get some rest."

Across the parade ground and near Los Moras Creek Rebecca sat on the porch of their home with Buff and the two children, Ben and Nicole. Rebecca looked up at the oaks that grew along the creek.

"He's been gone for a week Buff. Do you think everything is alright?"

"Now Rebecca," the old mountain man said, "You and I both kno that nutin' or no one cud keep that thar man of yurs from cuming back here to yu and them thar two kids. Why he'd fit tha devil his own self to git back here."

Rebecca smiled. "I love you old man. I don't know what Tye and I would have done if you hadn't showed up in our lives a few years ago." Buff fidgeted a little. "When Tye's gone you are such a comfort to have around and always just seem to know what to say when I get down and am missing Tye."

Buff chuckled. "Glad to kno I'm a kumfort."

Rebecca slapped him playfully on the shoulder. "You know what I mean. You…you're like a father to me; always near when I need someone to talk to, someone to lean on and tell my feelings to."

Buff put his arm around Rebecca's shoulders. "I tell yu sumthang Rebecca. I'd no family fur over fiftee years till yu and Tye tuk me in. I luv yu two like I wud luv my own kids ifin I'd ever had any." He chuckled and patted his Bowie named Susie that was always hanging in a beaded sheath on his belt. Thar ain't nutin in this here world that's means mor'n to me than Susie here cep' yu two."

Rebecca l said out loud. "Well I'm glad we mean more to you than that knife."

"Don't take it lightly lady. This here ole knife has dun me gud fur fortee or more yeers. Save'd my soree hide mor'n a few times. It's becum part uf me just like yu and Tye."

Rebecca shrugged off his arm and put hers around the small man and hugged him tight.

Buff patted her on the back. "Don't yu fret that purty head uf yourn nun. Tye's safe and will be back here reel soon. Yu'll see."

Tye sat on Sandy studying the land ahead. It was a lonely country. It wouldn't be in a few years, but for now there were few people unless one counted the Kiowa and the Comanche and they were a hell of lot less of them than a few short years ago. There were still enough of them around to make a white man be mighty thoughtful about where he went especially if he traveled alone. Southeast of here, Tye knew was the San Saba River and the Llano River Country, but he knew nothing about it other than what he had heard men say.

It was a rough country, rocky ground and hills, some being very steep with cliffs, scrub oak, cactus, cedars and mesquite. There were many draws that cut through the landscape from runoffs from the occasional storms that blew though over hundreds, maybe thousands of years. Tye patted Sandy on the neck. "It kinda looks our old stomping grounds Sandy except there's more water." Sandy snorted and nodded his big head. Tye chuckled. "I swear you understand everything I say don't you big boy." Sandy snorted and Tye laughed.

Tracking in this country was harder though because of the rocky terrain. Tye found a track here, a broken limb on a mesquite or cedar, sometimes it was just a rock that had been kicked out of place, but mostly it was just a feeling a man like Tye had to just know where the man he was trailing was going. He stayed on the breeds trail.

El Diablo squatted by a small spring cleansing the wound on his upper left arm. After washing it with water he walked to his saddlebag and took a bottle of whiskey and for the third time since being shot winced when he poured a little on the wound. Placing the bottle back in the bag he looked at his back trail for a moment.

For the first time since his parents had been killed he felt a little respect for another man.. This was no ordinary man. From what he had seen through the looking glass he was a big man, wore Apache style moccasin boots and his pants light blue with yellow stripe down the leg. The pants, the boots, big man, stays on a trail...*I have heard of such a man*, he thought, *but he was out of Fort Clark and stayed along the Border. That is a long ways from here. Watkins I think was his name. Big medicine among the Apache. No, he would not be way out here.*

He let his pony drink from the spring and then jumped in the saddle without using the stirrups. He took another quick look back in the direction he had come then headed due east with the sun setting behind him. He would find a place to camp and make plans for the gringo.

Sam had ridden hard since he had found Tye's trail. Tye was leaving a trial he could follow easily even sometimes making a little fun of Sam's tracking ability by leaving a arrow out of rocks or sticks pointing the way. The first time he found the marker he thought, *Always knew he was a smartass*! As he found new ones he just laughed.

Tye had travelled much slower since he was always searching for tracks or sign of a man passing and other times he would sit on Sandy and just put himself in the man's place he was after to see what he would do. This had worked countless times in the past and was something his pa had taught him to do… among a thousand other things.

It was going to be dark before long and no way did he want to try finding a man like he was following in the dark. He was anxious to end this thing, but he hadn't survived all these years chasing Apaches and outlaws by being foolish. He piled some white stones up in the shape of an arrow pointing to the left. He had seen a place along a cliff about fifty yards off the trail that looked like a good place to hole up for the night. The place had caught his eye because the vegetation was a little greener there than the area around it. "Might even be some water there boy," he said leading Sandy up the steep slope.

There was water-not much just a small pool of rain water in the shade of the overhang of the cliff. He filled his canteen and poured some into his hat and let Sandy have some. He refilled his canteen and then filled his coffee pot. He built a barrier of stones to hide the flames and then laid sticks and lit a small fire inside a circle of rocks. The circle and the barrier should keep the flame from prying eyes. He knew the man he was chasing was ahead of him, but he also knew he wasn't the only two legged varmint in this country and there was no sense advertising where his camp was.

Just before dark he heard horse hoofs hitting stones. He eased up and looked over the rocks he had piled up. He saw Sam looking at the stones he made the arrow from.

Sam looked up at the rim. "Come on up cowboy. Coffee's ready," he hollered. Sam dismounted and came up the slope leading his tired horse.

Tye met him and shook his hand. "Glad to see you Sam."

"Not half as glad as I am to see you," Sam said laughing.

"Take care of your horse and I'll get you a biscuit and some coffee." A few minutes later they were squatted by the fire sipping steaming hot coffee. "What about the kids?"

Sam took a sip of coffee before answering. "Found this couple named of Sam and Millie Matlock. They have one of the nicest homesteads I've been in. They will watch over them kids as if they were their own I can guarantee you that." He took another sip. "Now, what about Jed or El Diablo, or whatever he calls himself."

"He's ahead of us maybe an hour, maybe a little less."

Sam had a surprised look on his face. "That close?"

Tye nodded. "He laid up back a ways, waiting to ambush me and wasted a lot of time. Didn't work out for him the way he thought it would. He got a wounded shoulder out of it."

Sam looked at his partner and shook his head. "Don't guess you want to tell me about it?"

El Diablo

"Ain't much to tell Sam. He picked a spot that any man that has scouted Apaches like I have would have picked. It was a perfect ambush spot and I just guessed right."

"Yeah, right," Sam replied, a little sound of irritation in his voice. Once again Tye showed why he was so good at what he did. What amazed Sam was he was about the most modest, humble man he had ever met. Not one time in the two or so years that the two of them had trailed together had he patted himself on the back or bragged to anyone about what he had done over the years. Fact was when the talk turned to him he would change the subject or walk away. *If it was me I would probably add to the stories some and always save the pretty girl*, Sam thought to himself smiling. The fire was only coals now so both men rolled up in their bedrolls and was soon asleep.

Sam woke with a boot nudging his ribs. "Let's hit the leather. We ain't getting closer to the Breed staying here."

Chapter Seven

Several hours of steady riding brought the two men to the crest of a hill where they reined in their mounts looking at a cluster of what looked like new buildings. Tye looked down at the tracks. "He's headed for that town or what's supposed to be a town. You know the name?"

Sam thought for a moment. "Could be the new town of Brady City I heard about if that's the Brady Creek running by it. Not much is it?"

"Nope, but then towns aren't when they first start up. Let's head down there. That's where the tracks are headed."

Entering the outskirts of town they saw a cluster of men milling around in front of one of the buildings. As they rode up every man tuned their head looking their way and all talk ceased.

"Wonder what's going on?" Sam mumbled.

"Bet it has something to do with the Breed."

"What's all the excitement?" Sam asked as they stopped just short of the men.

"You rangers?" One man asked looking at the badges.

Tye leaned forward resting his hands on the pommel of his saddle. "Deputy United States Marshal's. This here is Sam Jenkins and I'm Tye Watkins."

Sam smiled knowing what was coming. Sure enough it did. "You the Tye Watkins from Fort Clark?" Tye nodded.

"Yes Sir. I was Chief of Scouts for a few years there."

"Can't be," another said. "I heard you were nine feet tall."

"Just a good example of why you don't believe half of what you hear about people," the Marshall replied smiling.

Then a voice came out of the crowd. "Hi Tye."

Tye looked at where the voice came from and was surprised to see a familiar face. "Private Cribs. What are you doing here? I thought you were still at Clark." He dismounted and walked to the man as men stepped aside. The two men shook hands.

"I got out about a month ago and heard about this new town being built so I thought I'd come here and try to fit in." He turned to the men and spoke in a loud voice. "All the stories you have heard about this man are true. When trouble comes, he's a one man army. He killed more Apaches by the time he was eighteen than all of you put together in your lives. Now he and his partner Sam there are putting the fear of God in the outlaws around here."

"God only knows we need some help," A man said in the crowd drawing some laughter.

"A good man was killed earlier Tye," Cribs said. "Gunned down in cold blood before two other men."

"What men?" Tye said looking around.

"Me and Billy Waites, Marshal," a man said stepping from the crowd and extending his hand. "I'm George Milburn."

Tye shook the man's hand. "What happened?"

"Me, Billy, and James Langley, that's James lying over there, were sitting on the porch when the man rode into town and walked his horse up to the rail there and went inside. We were talking about what a bad hombre he looked like when he came out with a sack of supplies. He got in the saddle and started to ride off when the owner of the store stepped out holding his bloody head where the man had hit him with his pistol. James stood up and hollered at the man to hold up and before anyone could say anything else or even move the stranger had pulled his gun and shot James right thru the head and lit a shuck out of town."

"That's the truth Marshal," a man said a bloody bandage showing beneath his hat. "He came into my store picked up some items and asked me to put them into a sack for him. I did and he started to leave when I asked him about paying for them. He said he didn't need money when he had this and pulled his gun and hit me in the head with it."

Tye looked at the man. "We've been trailing him for awhile. You're lucky mister since you're the only man he's come across he hasn't killed." Tye looked at Cribbs. "How long ago did this happen?"

"Maybe an half a hour ago."

"Damn, we're closer than we thought Tye. Let' go."

Tye had his hand on the pommel ready to mount when a voice boomed out from behind the men. "So you are the great Tye Watkins, Injun killer and hunter of men. The great Texas hero and savior of the people along the Border. I think you are a piece of horse shit."

"Who is that Cribs?" Tye asked.

"Larry Wurth, son of a large rancher and thinks he's the fastest gun in Texas."

Tye looked at the youngster. "Why don't you just get along home to your mommy son and leave me alone." Tye turned to mount Sandy.

"Just what I figured Watkins. You're afraid to face a real man."

Tye turned slowly around and men backed up. "I hear you and your family have a ranch. That right?'

"So."

"I just wanted to make sure you had a place to be buried and by people who cared for you, son. Man shouldn't die and no one to care or mourn over him."

"You gonna talk me to death."

"If I can't talk you out of it, make your play.' Tye watched the man's face. When he saw the man's eyes narrow he knew he was going to draw. As the young man's hand flashed down to his gun Tye drew and fired. The slug hit the man's shoulder just as his gun cleared leather and then clattered to the floor. A look of astonishment showed on the youngsters face.

"I...I didn't see your hand move," he said holding his shoulder with his left hand blood trickling down through his fingers.

Tye walked over to the young man and looked at his shoulder. "Go back to ranching son and live a long life. You're way to slow to make it long as a gunslinger. By rights, I could have killed you and no one would say it wasn't self defense. Another man might have."

He turned to walk away when the kid said. "Mr. Watkins-thanks." Tye walked through the men and mounted Sandy. He turned to the men.

"We'll get the man who killed James. You have a good man among you in Cribs there. He'll fit in fine if you will let him and if trouble comes, let him help you take care of it." He tipped his hat with his right hand and the two lawmen rode off leaving Cribs to answer a lot of questions about what he knew of Tye.

Out of town they reined their mounts in to a trot. Sam looked at Tye. "That's the start of it."

"Start of what."

"Your reputation as a fast draw. Word will get around about that incident just you wait and see."

Tye paid no attention as he reined in sharply and dismounted. "What's wrong Tye?"

"Saw some tracks leading off the road-fresh tracks." He looked in the direction they led and suddenly hollered at Sam to get down quick. Sam swung his leg over just as a bullet cut the air where he had been an instant before. He fell off his horse and scrambled to where Tye was behind a thick cedar.

"Damn-that was close," he swore. "What did you see?"

"I looked to where the tracks were heading and saw a flash of sunlight off something. Not much in nature that reflects sunlight so I figured it was a rifle barrel."

"Where's the dry gulching son-of-a-bitch at?"

"In those boulder up there to the left of the stand of cedars."

"If you hadn't seen those tracks leaving the road one or both of us would be deader than a piece of drift wood."

Tye was trying to come up with a plan to get out of this fix they were in. There was no cover close except this cedar they were behind and to try to move would be suicide. That's when they heard the sound of horse's hooves striking rocks.

He's on the move, Sam. Get to the horses." Both men jumped up and in two strides were at their mounts and leaped into the saddles not bothering with the stirrups and reining them up the slope to where the Breed had been. It was a struggle for the horses because of the loose rock and steep incline. When they had covered the hundred yards and crested the hill the horses were breathing hard. They just got a glimpse of El Diablo as he rounded a hill about a quarter mile off running his mount hard.

"Let's go," yelled Sam and then quickly looked at Tye as he had grabbed Sam's mounts reins. "What are you doing?"

"The horses need to catch their breath after that climb, Sam. They won't make it two miles if you run them hard now and where will you be then with no horse."

Sam started to argue, but he knew Tye was right. Tye released the reins and both men let their mounts walk easy down the slope and then at the bottom, nudged them into an easy trot.

"Damn him to hell," the Breed cursed. "That son-of-a-bitch has to be Watkins. Ain't no other white man would have smelled that trap. He looked over his shoulder and seeing no one slowed his horse to an easy gallop and after a few minutes to a trot then a walk. He was a hard man, a cruel man who had no qualms about killing another man-or woman for that matter. He was a man driven to revenge for what had been done to him and it made no difference to him the men and women he killed had nothing to do with the killing of his parents and family. He was alone in the world-no friends and no family and he liked it that way. He had gone from a peaceable family man to what he was now in a short period of time. He was El Diablo, the one called the devil, and he would kill and kill and kill as long as blood flowed through his veins.

McMillan

I will take extra pleasure in killing this man Watkins if that is who he is. He thought to himself. *He is a great warrior I hear and a hero to the people.* He spit into the dirt beside his horse. *I spit on you Watkins. You will be food for the buzzards soon.* He nudged his horse into a gallop.

El Diablo

Chapter Eight

The two lawmen made a camp just before full dark. They were close behind the killer but neither wanted to stumble into him in the dark. He would be expecting them and one or both of them could be killed. The trail of the outlaw was heading straight for the town of Fredericksburg, a small town that was settled in the mid 1840's by a people of mostly German ancestry. Tye knew nothing about it other than he had heard that the Confederate soldiers had massacred a large number of German settlers in what was known as the Nueces Massacre in 1862.

"Town was named for a named for a man by the name of Prince Frederick who helped settled the town in about 1846 or so," Sam said as they drank coffee and chewed on biscuits and jerky. "I think I heard he was from some country called Prussia or something like that. The population is mostly men and women of German blood but they are a few Mexicans and Americans there also."

"I thought all of us living in Texas were Americans," Tye mumbled while chewing a biscuit.

"Hell, we are Tye. I was making a point of the different bloodlines that are there."

"Oh," Tye said laughing loudly.

"Smart ass," Sam chuckled realizing Tye was just trying to get a rise out of him. "Where you going," he asked when Tye stood up.

"Going to work on my draw some," Tye answered. He walked a few feet away and for five solid minutes drew his Colt, reholstered it and drew again over and over.

. "Gawd Almighty Tye," Sam exclaimed. "That was quicker than a rattler's strike."

"Getting better all the time. The gunsmith in Brackett did a lot for me when he worked over the gun. He fixed the firing mechanism to where you just have to breathe on the trigger for it to fire and removing the front sight makes it smoother coming out of the leather."

"Well you're damn sure the fastest I ever saw and I've seen a few."

"I figure it will come in handy some day."

"Men wanting a reputation will be coming for you Tye. Men don't do what you did today with that kid. He was going to kill you Tye as will the others. Shoot to kill not wound the man. You're good but if you had missed today would you have had time to shoot again before he blasted you to hell. My pa, who was also handy with a gun, always told me to make the first shot at the body because that's the biggest target."

"That's something to think about," Tye said.

"Well, if that time comes don't let your thinking get in the damn way. I sure would hate to have to take care of that purty wife of yours if you get yourself killed," he said laughing.

Tye laughed and then said, "Let's get some shuteye."

Tye woke up and looked at the stars. From their position he figured it was about one o'clock. He sat up and pulled on his moccasin boots he had taken out of the saddle bags before lying down.

"What are you doing?" Sam asked in a low voice.

"See if I can find his camp and maybe surprise him."

""I'll go to," Sam said throwing off his blanket.

"No, Sam." Tye said placing his hand on his friends shoulder and pushing him back on his bedroll. "Stay here with the horses. He knows we are behind him and he may try to do what I'm doing, sneak up on us and kill us while we sleep. Just stay awake and watch the horses. They will alert you if anyone or anything is out there. I'll be back in an hour or two. I don't figure he's more than a mile or so from here. I'll holler and let you know it's me coming but if you don't hear me and something moves shoot it to hell."

Tye was gone, moving like a ghost making no sound. *Damn! If that Breed moves like that how am I going to hear him?* Sam thought for a moment and then got up and found a couple of dead limbs and laid them on the blankets. He then spread another blanket over each limb. He took off his hat and placed it so it looked like it was over his face while he slept and then backed off away from the camp and sat with his back to a large boulder next to the horses. He looked at the camp. It looked as if two men were sleeping. He had his Colt in his hand and despite the coolness of the night, he was sweating.

Tye moved slowly, careful not to step on anything like a stone that could roll and make a noise or a small branch off a mesquite or cedar that might snap and sound like a gunshot in the stillness of the early morning. He had walked, crawled, and scooted on his belly for close to an hour when he spotted the coals of the small fire. He crawled a few feet closer and studied the camp. Nothing, not even a bed roll was to be seen nor Jeb's horse. "Too late, he's already gone. Damn him to h..." Tye's cursing was interrupted by the faint sound of several gunshots. "Damn him," Tye cursed as he started running back toward his camp and Sam.

An hour passed since Tye left and as hard as Sam tried fatigue and need for sleep was settling upon him. He caught himself a couple of time nodding off and silently cursed his self for doing so. A horse nickered and he was alert. Looking around he strained his eyes looking thru the darkness. He heard no sound, nothing at all which told him something was out there. He looked at the horses and as he did, Sandy nickered and his ears twitched. Sam looked in the direction Sandy was looking and as he did the stillness of the night was suddenly shattered by the sound of shots being fired into what was supposedly sleeping men. Sam jumped up and fired his Colt at the flashes and then felt a blow to his left arm and he dropped to the ground and continued firing till his colt fell on an empty chamber. He quickly fed new shells into the gun and waited. Two minutes later He heard Tye yell.

"Sam, you okay?"

"Yeah, just a scratch. Best be careful he's still out there somewhere laying for us."

"He's gone," Tye answered walking into the camp. He hurried over to Sam. "Hit bad."

"Nah," Sam said

"Let me take a look," Tye said. "Take your shirt off." Sam did and Tye looked at the wound which was just a crease that barely trickled blood. "Hold still while get some stuff from my saddlebags." Tye came back with a piece of cloth for a bandage and a surprise in his hand. He poured the whiskey on the wound.

Sam jerked and stood up. "Son-of-a-bi…. You could have warned me."

"And spoil my fun of watching you holler like a little kid," Tye chuckled remembering the time Captain McClellan poured whiskey on one of his wounds. The soldiers in the camp that night howled with laughter as Tye jumped around hollering and swearing.

"Looks like he wanted it to end here," Tye said holding up one of the blankets with two holes in it. "Heard his Henry and some shots from a Colt. Did you hit him?"

"I fired at the flashes from his rifle. Don't know if I hit him or not."

He'll probably be moving on tonight. We can't follow in the dark so let's rest up some and get a early start. He probably won't risk coming back here tonight, but we won't take any chances," Tye said putting the small fire out. He then brought the horses in a little closer and picketed them knowing there was no better sentry than them.

Jeb had made it back to his camp and before saddling his horse and putting the camp in order he wrapped a kerchief around the crease in his left shoulder. He was worried, not scared, but worried that this man was actually better than him. *He seems to know what I am* going *to do before I do,* he thought. *This is what I had heard about him from the Apache. He was a man of his word who was respected by the Apache. He was also feared by them because he was the one white man who could think like they thought, if need be live off the land like they did, tracked as well or better than their best tracker, and no one was a better warrior. High praise coming from an Apache for a white man.* He considered all these thing as he rode toward the town of Fredericksburg. *This thinking, this knowing what I am going to do before I do it could work against him and for me if I can think of a way to trick him.* He was in thought the rest of the day. He was making his trail hard to follow by changing directions, using rocky ground, dragging brush behind his horse and once, finding a small stream walked his horse in it for over a mile before leaving it. It was dusk when he saw the outskirts of Fredericksburg.

A man with a derby hat, striped shirt and baggy pants banged on the piano loudly, but not very well. The patrons in the saloon however was paying little attention to Jeb as they were engrossed mostly with drinking, playing cards or watching card games that were going on at several tables. They paid no attention to the man standing just inside the batwing doors of the saloon looking things over. Satisfied no one was in the room that he knew Jed walked to the bar.

The bartender came over wearing what once was a white apron and wiping a shot glass with a dirty towel. "What will it be strang…" he stopped in mid sentence when he saw the man up close. He looked at the long black hair that hung to the man's shoulder, the hat with an eagle feather, and the dark complexion. "We don't serve Injuns or breeds in here mister," he growled. Several heads turned at the remark.

"I have money,"Jeb said.

"I don't want your damn money," the bartender said his voice rising so now everyone in the saloon was looking, listening. "I said we don't serve no stinking Injuns and sure as hell no breeds in here. Now get the hell out."

What happened next happened so quick no one had time to react. The Breeds left hand shot forward and his hand grabbed the back of the bartender's neck and he slammed the man's face down hard on the hard oak top of the bar. You could hear the bones break in the man's nose and blood spurted everywhere. The bartender jumped back holding his smashed nose with his left hand and reaching for the shotgun with his right. The gun was just coming to the top of the bar when a knife thrown by the Breed stuck in his chest to the hilt just below the top button on his shirt. The shotgun clattered to the wooden floor as the bartender fell backwards grabbing a shelf and pulling it and all the bottles of whiskey down with him.

When the men realized what happened some started toward the breed, but stopped in their tracks as a Colt suddenly materialized in the man's hand.

"He can't shoot us all," a man hollered and then died as a 45 slug tore into his chest just about where his heart was located. The batwings flew open and a man rushed in.

"What's the ruckus about?" He shouted and then died as a heavy slug put a hole thru the tin star on his chest. Breed swung the gun back on the other men.

El Diablo

"Anyone else want to die?" No one moved. "Didn't think so," he said and picked up the mug of beer the man next to him was drinking and downed it. "All I wanted was a beer. No need for all this here trouble if he had sold me one. "You," he said pointing at an old man. "Get my knife out that bastard's chest and clean it off on his apron then hand it to me real careful like. The man did as he was told and handed the knife to Breed and stepped back. "Now old man, pour me a beer." The man did as he was told and Jeb drank the beer watching the men as he did. Finishing his beer, Breed replaced the knife in the sheath and backing toward the door said, "Wouldn't be smart to stick your head out that door for a few minutes. " He backed on out the door and grabbing his horses reins swung into the saddle not bothering with using the stirrups. He fired a shot thru the doors for good measure and reined his mount out of town the opposite way he had came in. He was out of town by the time anyone was brave enough to stick his head out.

Tye and Sam rode into Fredericksburg shortly after the sun was half way across its journey to the western hills. They had lost a lot of time trying to keep on the Breeds trail. The man was as good as any Apache Tye had tracked at keeping his trail covered. They rode down the street until they saw the sheriff's office and reined in there. A man was sweeping off the porch

"Sheriff in?" Sam asked.

"Nope," the man answered without looking up.

"Where can we find him then?"

"Who's asking? The man asked still sweeping.

Sam, becoming a little irritated at the man said in a tone that got the man's attention. "US Deputies Sam Jenkins and Tye Watkins."

The man stopped his sweeping and looked up. "Why didn't you say so in the first place? Sheriff was shot earlier. "Say, did you say your name was Tye Watkins?"

Sam, used to people asking that question replied. "No, my partner here is Tye Watkins and yes before you ask, he's the scout from Fort Clark that everyone in Texas has heard about," he added smiling, the anger tone in his voice at the man gone.

The man dropped the broom and walked past Sam and his horse and reached up and stuck out his hand which Tye took. "Right proud to meet you Mr. Watkins. I had a son who was in the Calvary at Clark. He was killed there fighting Apaches. Told me a lot about you in the letters we got."

"What was his name?" Tye asked.

"Christian…Sergeant James Christian."

"Well I be damned," Tye swore. "You're Sergeant Christian's father." The old man nodded. Tye stepped down from Sandy. "Your son was one of best friends and one of the top soldiers I ever had the privilege of knowing."

"Thank you for that Tye. I sorter figured that from his letters me and ma received. He spoke of you in a way that I figured ya'll were more than just soldier boy and scout that happened to be on patrol together every once in awhile."

Tye put his hand on the man's shoulder. "Maybe after we see the sheriff we can have a beer together."

"I shore nuff like that Tye, but there's one problem; the sheriff is dead." Tye and Sam looked at each other. "He was killed along with two other men by a man the witnesses said was a breed."

"What happened?" Sam asked dismounting from his horse.

"The way I heard it was that Rufus, he was the bartender, refused to serve this man a beer on account of his being part injun. The man took offense and slammed poor old Rufus's face on the bar and when Rufus reached for the shotgun under the bar the man threw a knife quicker than a rattlers strike. He shot a man who was telling everyone he was only one man and to get him. About that time the Sheriff came busting through the door to see what was going on and the man shot him. Put that bullet right thru the tin star on his chest. Then asked if anyone else wanted to die just move an inch. He told them not to come out the door or he would blow their head off-they believed him.

Tye shook his head. "He's a bad one Mr. Christian. Been killing men and women for awhile in Mexico and in

Texas. We need some supplies before we go on. Where's a good place to get stocked up?"

"Right down the street on your left is the mercantile store."

"Tye," the old man said. "Afore you go can you answer a question for me?" Tye looked at his friend's father and took a gold piece out of his shirt pocket and handed it to Sam.

"Get us some supplies Sam while I visit a minute with Mr. Christian. I'll be along in a minute or two." Sam nodded, tipped his hat to the old man and headed down the street.

"The onliest question I have Tye is how my boy died. The letter just said he was killed in action against the Apache. How did he die Tye?"

Tye bowed his head and a lump formed in his throat remembering that day when his friends Sergeant Christian and Lieutenant Garrison and lot of other good men died. "It's sorter hard for me to talk about that day Mr. Christian. I lost two good friends that day, your son and Lieutenant Garrison." He paused for a few seconds gathering his thoughts. "It was one of the largest battles we had fought at the time as far as the numbers involved of both soldiers and Apaches. Your son and a number of soldiers were caught in a hand to hand fight with an overwhelming number of Apaches. That is the worse situation a soldier can be in because no one is better than the Apache in that situation. Sergeant Christian's horse was shot and when he stumbled and fell your son's leg was pinned under the horse and he could not get free of the weight. He died fighting like he always did-like a man obsessed. They found him with four dead Apaches lying around him with one on top of him with your sons hands around his throat. He was a top soldier and one greatly respected and loved by the other men. He was my friend and there's not a day goes by that I don't miss him."

Tears ran down the old man's wrinkled face. He was a little shamed and quickly wiped the tears away. "Man ought not to do that," he said, "especially after all this time."

"Ain't no shame in showing emotion Mr. Christian. I wouldn't think much of a man who didn't."

The old man nodded. "You're right about that. You're a fine example of a man Tye. I can see why my son thought so highly of you. I can't wait to tell Ma about meeting you."

"You take care sir and you and your wife go on with the knowledge your son was respected and loved by a lot of good men and he died like a soldier doing what he loved to do. He loved the Calvary." He reached out and shook the old man's hand. "If I get back through here I would love to meet your wife."

"We'll look forward to it, Tye."

Tye mounted Sandy and walked him to the mercantile store just as Sam came out with the supplies. "Ready to ride?"

Sam nodded, tied the saddle bags on behind the cantle of his saddle and then toeing the stirrup swung into the saddle. He wiggled his butt a few times into a comfortable position in the saddle and nudged his horse into a trot. They rode just off the road on opposite sides looking for tracks leaving the road.

Tye was doing a lot of thinking. Thinking of another man he had know who had as little regard for another's life as the man they were after now. *Yancey Cates, he thought, was the worse that God could create. He had been a man with a twisted mind, almost crazy along with his brother. This man known as El Diablo was as bad-maybe worse. Been thinking on him and remembered rumor has it his family was killed by Mexicans while he was away so I can understand his feelings about what happened to his family and maybe just a little feeling for what he has done, but it was Mexicans that killed his family not the white folks he has been killing and most of the Mexicans he has killed knew nothing about his families killing. He is just a good man probably at one time that fate has turned him into a mad man, a man living for one thing and that's killing as long as he breathes.*

"Here Tye," Sam said reining his mount in and stepping down from the saddle. "Tracks leading off the road," he said pointing to the ground. Tye dismounted and knelt by the tracks studying them closely.

"It's him," Tye said. "His horse's left front hoof is slightly turned in," he said tracing the hoof print with his finger. Western men, at least those men who like Tye that had spent their life hunting for food or tracking Apaches or hunting down outlaws had an ability to remember a horses hoof prints as easily as he could remember a man's face. No two horses have the same stride or maybe just have a shoe that had a crack or chip in it. A man could tell if the horse was in need of shoes or had just been shod or in this case had a foot that was slightly turned in. The more experienced could tell after following a particular horse for awhile if the horse was carrying a man or a woman or no one by the depth of his print in the ground. He could tell if it was lame or if worn out and about ready to cave in. A man could learn a lot about the rider by his horse's tracks.

"I see," Sam said but not really understanding the lesson he had just been given.

Tye stood up. "Tracks are headed west."

"Not much out there that way," Sam noted. He stood with his hands on the pommel of his saddle staring in the direction the tracks headed thinking of what lay in that direction other than Mexico and that was a hundred and fifty or more miles. There were a few small towns in that direction and a few forts including Fort Clark and Camp Wood but a lot of distance between them. It wouldn't be hard to pass through undetected.

Tye walked a few steps and picked up a piece of cloth with red stains on it. He placed the cloth under his nose and sniffed. "Blood, Sam. One of us has put a bullet in him or at least nicked him some."

"To bad it wasn't between the eyes. I got me a feeling this is going to get nasty pretty damn quick."

They mounted and Tye led off following the tracks and thinking about what Sam just said. "Probably right about that Sam. I've been thinking the same thing myself. He looked at the terrain all about him as he trotted Sandy and then looked to the horizon. Nothing moved nor even a sound: no birds chirping, no small animals scurrying about, not even a buzzard overhead. He reined Sandy in and just sat there studying the lay of the lay.

"What is it Tye?"

"Look around and then tell me what you see or hear."

A minute later Sam said. "I don't see anything nor hear anything."

"Don't you find that a little unusual?"

"Now that you mention it, yeah. What do you make of it?"

"What you said awhile ago about things getting nasty pretty soon, I think it's that time." He nodded toward the trail ahead. The tracks led into a narrow canyon that even to Sam looked dangerous as hell. It was maybe a hundred fifty yards wide with steep walls that were almost a hundred feet high in places. Every where a man looked he saw a dozen places a shooter could hide. There was little brush on the walls but ledges, crevices, and shallow caves where the rock had gave way and fell down to the canyon floor. Here and there along the bottom were mesquites and sage that offered a little shade- and concealment for someone who didn't want to be seen. *Just about as dangerous place as I have ever seen*, Tye was thinking. He looked at Sam. "Ride easy and ready." He took his Henry out of its leather and laid it across his saddle, his finger on the trigger and the hammer back. Sam did the same. "Rein up beside me and watch the left wall and I'll watch the right. You see anything, yell and get out of the saddle quick."

El Diablo

Sam rode up beside him and they started to slowly make their way through the canyon.

Sam was sweating profusely and the salt was burning his eyes. Wrapping the reins around the pommel of his saddle and using his left hand he removed his kerchief and wiped the sweat from his forehead and eyes not taking his finger of his right hand off the trigger of his Henry rifle for even a second. He risked taking a quick look at Tye. *Damn man must have ice in his veins not appearing nervous at a stinking time like this. This is horse dung waiting for someone to take a shot at you so then your partner will know where he is while you lay dead in the damn dirt. Look at him: I'm about to wet my pants and he's just a sitting there looking around like he's on a Sunday stroll. Hell even my horse don't like this for crap*, he thought as his horse blew and shook his head.

He was startled when Tye laughed. "He's not in the canyon Sam. I guessed he learned his lesson."

"What lesson?"

"We're smart enough to know an ambush spot so he's gonna pick a place that's not obvious, one that a man would not even notice."

"Oh, that's supposed to be funny."

"Not really, but at least we're into his head a little and I guarantee he's a little nervous."

"That's good to know that I'm not the only one that's about to dirty his pants," Sam mumbled.

The looked at him and smiled. "Was a little nerve wracking there for a while wasn't it?"

"A little nerve wracking ain't exactly how I would put it pard."

Tye chuckled and looked at the tracks. "He's trotting his horse so let's close the gap some. He nudged Sandy into an easy lope. He kept his eyes on the tracks as well as the terrain. The horses could hold this pace for a long time and maybe speed up the end of this chase.

El Diablo

Chapter Nine

Darkness was a short time away and still no sign of Jeb. Tye reined in Sandy. "We had better find a place to camp. We can't follow him at night and I sure as hell don't want to stumble into him accidently like." They rode for another ten minutes before Tye spotted what he was looking for; a cut in the canyon wall that was fifteen or so feet wide and extended far enough back they could picket their horses. There was a good field of fire in front and darkness would prevent a shooter from being able to hit anything from the high walls of the canyon. It would be full dark by the time they set up camp and cared for the horses and would leave out before daylight so he felt pretty secure in this place.

Tye built a small fire banking it with rocks to hide the flames. He put on some coffee and put some bacon in the frying pan while Sam cared for the horses. By the time Sam was through they had coffee, bacon and some hard biscuits they soaked in the bacon grease. They sat cross legged around the fire eating and drinking the coffee which was strong enough to float a spoon which meant is was good cowboy coffee.

After some small talk Tye suggested they get some shut eye since he felt like tomorrow the book would be closed on the man called El Diablo-one way or another. He sat for a few minute listening for sounds that after long years of experience he knew were the normal sounds of the night; the flapping of a bats wings as they searched for insects to eat, the sound of small animals such as pack rats and field mice scurrying among the rocks, the noise of a owls wings as he swooped over the camp, and always the lonely wail of a coyote howling at the moon or whatever they howled at plus other sounds like the night breeze rustling the leaves of the bushes. Any sound other than the normal sounds would awake him instantly. He was accustomed to noticing the lay of the land around him before dark and did this without thinking about it. It was one of the thousand things his pa had taught him and was one of things he did without thinking.

"Always study the things around you before you make camp. Notice the trees, bushes, and rocks and how they stand or lay. Things look different after dark and can spook a man if he don't know what he is looking at especially with a full moon casing shadows as it moves across the sky," pa would say when they made camp.

El Diablo

They were moving just as it was light enough to see. An hour later they found where Jeb had camped. He had found a spot that was surrounded by thick brush with only an opening barely wide enough for a horse to pass through. One way in and one way out. Tye knew by the horse droppings that he had picketed his horse in the opening to alert him if anything or anyone tried to get past him. The brush everywhere else was thick enough that even an Apache would not be able to get through it without making noise. They picked up his trail and continued the chase.

Tye realized quickly that the trail was different. Jeb was making no effort to cover his tracks or slow them down by taking to rocky ground or staying in the water and going up or down stream in a couple of small creeks they had crossed. He took his Henry out of its leather and laid it across the saddle so it would be handy. Sam noticed and did the same. He had been riding with Tye for almost two years and had learned a lot about tracking and reading signs of trouble from the ex-scout. He was reading trouble now.

They came to a fairly wide shallow river and followed the tracks into it and out the other side. Tye reined Sandy in and sat there for a moment reading the lay of the land.

"Do you know where we are Sam?"

"Not exactly but I figure we are north and a little ways west of Uvalde. This is probably the Nueces River if I was guessing."

"This is the Nueces. I recognize it from the time I was here before probably three or four years ago chasing a man named Carter. We were trapped by Comanche's about a mile south of here. Carter left us and brought back a patrol from Fort Inge to run off the Comanche and saved our bacon. Carter was given the choice of going to prison or joining the U.S. Calvary. He joined up and become a top soldier and good friend. He's a sergeant last I heard."

They rode on following the tracks and Tye nudged Sandy into an easy lope again since the tracks were easy enough to follow. He was excited now not only because they were close to the man they had been trailing for over a week but they were within forty five miles or less of Fort Clark and Rebecca and the kids. After thirty minutes he slowed Sandy to a walk. They were approaching the mountains north of Fort Clark. At least they were mountains to him. Old Buff laughed at what us Texans called mountains saying they would only be foothills to the Rockies. He would say that "them thar montons in tha Rockies wur so tall tha wud tetch tha sky." He smiled at the thought of his old friend and the way he talked. Buff had spent a lot of time telling stories about his time in the Rockies with Jim Bridger and Tye's pa trapping beaver.

Tye knew that the next few miles until they passed through these hills were going to be dangerous. Every step could lead them into a bullet from behind some rock, tree or bush. He also knew it was going to be slow going because the rocky ground would naturally make it harder to read sign. Sam knew they could be in trouble by just reading Tye and realizing the man was more alert than he had been which told Sam he had better be ready for trouble.

El Diablo

Suddenly Tye shouted "SAM!" Tye saw the flash of sunlight and knew it was a rifle and started to throw himself from the saddle but he was not quick enough. He felt the blow to his head and knew he was falling and then nothing.

Sam had thrown himself clear of the saddle just as a second bullet cut the air where he had been. He hit the rocky ground hard and rolled as another bullet kicked up the dirt where he had just been an instant before. He rolled again and then was behind a boulder. Bullets struck the face of the boulder and whined off into the air. Sam looked at the still form of Tye stretched out on the ground not moving. Tears welled up in his eyes at the thought of his friend dead and then anger-anger like he had never known before swelled up inside of him. He knew his friend was dead because he had turned to warn him before he jumped from the saddle and that delay was why he was hit.

"You son-of-a-bitch," he yelled and stood up firing his Henry at the spot where he had seen the smoke as fast as he could work the leaver and pull the trigger. He saw the flash and smoke from the rifle to the left of where he was shooting at and felt a blow to his left shoulder knocking him to the ground. He lay there not moving anything except his eyes. *Should have known a fighting man like him wouldn't stay in one spot,* he thought as he watched the slope in front of him.

A minute later he saw the man stand up and start down the hill toward him. He watched, waited. Just a little closer, he thought. Just come a little closer. His left arm was numb and he wasn't sure he could move it. Shock so far had not let the pain set in, but it would soon enough. He had been shot before and knew sometimes it was a few minutes before the pain set in. When Jeb had his head down for a second watching his footing on the slippery slope Sam moved slightly to get his rifle in position.

Jeb was elated. He had killed the great Watkins and the deputy too. "You don't look so tough now Watkins. Just fresh meat for the buzzards to feast on," he said to himself as he moved down the slope, a grin covering his face in anticipation of scalping the great scout. His grin faded when he saw the deputy move and bring his rifle up. Jeb fired quickly, too quick and knew he had missed. He saw the rifle belch fire and smoke and felt the slug hit him spinning him around.   He was quickly on his feet and fired again at the deputy and saw his bullet knock the man's leg out from under him, but the gringo was firing his rifle and slugs were whistling by his head and others kicking up dirt in front of him. He ran as he had never run before. His lungs were about to burst when he finally rounded the hill and out of the deputy's vision. He stopped running and tried to catch his breath knowing the man was in no shape to follow him. He walked up the hill to his horse and sat down. That's when the pain hit him. The shock of the slug and the adrenalin rush of battle and having killed Watkins wore off. He sat down and opened his shirt. The bullet had hit him in the side just above the hip bone and exited out his back. He took off his shirt and wrapped it tight around his waist hoping the pressure would stem the flow of blood. He knew infection would probably set in if he didn't see a doctor and the closest one was in Brackett. He struggled and finally and painfully got on his horse and headed him southwest toward Brackett and Fort Clark.

El Diablo

Sam crawled over to his friend and saw the blood on the ground by his head. He knew Tye was dead and he lay there grieving over his friend. Five, ten minutes passed and he finally raised his head and moved his good arm to turn Tye over. As he did he was shocked when a groan came from Tye.

"He's alive!" he shouted. "God in Heaven he's alive." He crawled up beside Tye and saw the wound, a cut along the side of his head just above the ear. The bullet had just grazed his head. He whistled at Sandy. "Come here boy, come here," he said. Sandy walked over and stood over Tye. He lowered his head and gave Tye a nudge in the side. Tye moaned again. Holding onto the reins Sam pulled himself up and leaned against the saddle for a minute to let the dizziness pass. When things stopped spinning he grabbed the canteen off the saddle and dropped to the ground screaming in pain from his leg and shoulder.

He pulled the cork on the canteen and poured a little water on Tye's face. Tye's eyes opened for a second and then closed. He poured a little more water and Tye opened his eyes and looked around.

"Wh..what happened Sam?'

You've been shot Tye. You took a bullet alongside your head and you've been out."

"Where's Jeb, "Tye asked holding his hand to his head. He looked at his hand which had came away bloody.

"He got away. But I hit him pretty good. He's damn sure hurting."

"How come you're not after him, pard?"

"I'm pretty shot up Tye. Sure ain't in no shape to go chasing anyone."

Tye rose up on one elbow and then lowered his head back down. "Give me a minute Sam to let the world stop spinning and I'll take a look." He took a small swallow of water and then poured a little on his face. He rose up more slowly this time and looked over Sam's wounds. "You're not going to die from these wounds Sam, but you're going to be laid up for a spell. We need to get you to Clark and the doctor so no infection sets in."

"What about your head?" Sam asked grimacing as a wave of pain rocked his body.

"I've had worse," Tye answered removing his kerchief and wrapping it around his head. He stood slowly up and opened one of the saddle bags and removed a bottle of rot gut. He took a swig and felt the burn in his throat and belly and felt a little better. He kneeled beside Sam. "This is going to hurt some," and poured a little whiskey on each wound, both the entry and where each bullet exited. Sam hollered like a woman in labor cussing Tye and calling him names Tye had never heard before.

Tye stood up slowly holding onto his saddle and took a shirt from his other saddle bag and with his Bowie cut it into strips. Neither wound was bleeding much so he just wrapped them tightly and hoped they would not start again.

"I hate to do this pard, but I'm going to have to get you on your horse. We can make it to Clark by noon tomorrow if we ride straight through. I could make a travois but it would take longer to get there and you need medical help quick."

"Just get me on. I'll stay in the saddle."

A couple minutes later and after a lot of groaning and cussing Sam was in the saddle. Tye mounted Sandy and they moved off. Tye's head hurt with Sandy's every step, but he knew his hurt was nothing like Sam's. He handed Sam the bottle. "Drink some of this and maybe it will help with the pain." Sam took the bottle and took a hefty swig.. Then he took another and another and pretty soon most of the pain had stopped. Tye noticed him swaying in the saddle so he halted Sandy and dismounted. He took some rope and cut it into a piece long enough to tie Sam's hands to the pommel on the saddle and then cut another long enough to tie one boot and go under the horses belly and tied the other end to his other boot. He pulled the rope tight and Sam wasn't going to fall off. Sam giggled.

"What's so funny?"

"You, Tye," he answered his words slurred by the whiskey. "Your hat is all cockeyed."

Tye smiled knowing his hat sat sideways on his head because of the kerchief. Tye remounted and started off again at a brisk pace. His thoughts went to the type of men out here like Sam and Sergeant Arnold. back at Clark. This land is rough, open country and takes a different kind of man than what one would find back east in the cities. Some men in the big cities never discover what they can do when the chips are down, what they have inside, but out here a man has to be a man or he just ain't going to make it. In the cities you have other men to lean on and you have officers of the law to take care of situations. Out here a man learns to take care of his own problems, fight his own battles. You hide from an enemy or back down from a fight out here, word gets around and people think of you as a coward and a coward out here is the worse handle that can be put on a man. He looked back at Sam who was singing some unknown tune and singing it badly. It takes men like Sam there to make this country into what it can be.

They rode through the rest of the day and night stopping only briefly three times to water and give the horses a blow. Mid morning had them within sight of Brackett and Fort Clark and a deadly surprise.

Chapter 10

"What the hell happened to you, Tye?" The guard at the gate asked. He then looked at Sam who was passed out with his chin resting on his chest. "Is that Sam? He looks in a bad way," noticing the bloody bandages

"Yeah, that's Sam and he's in a bad way. We're heading to see old Sawbones at the hospital and get fixed up then I'm going to see Rebecca and the kids for awhile.

A voice rang out from up the road toward headquarters. "Is that you Tye, you old Warhorse?"

"It's me Arnold or at least what's left anyway, Tye replied smiling at his old friend Sergeant Arnold. Arnold turned and hollered at a private and told him to tell the surgeon that he had some business coming his way.

"What the hell happened to you two," Arnold asked looking at Sam?"

"It's a long story Arnold. Let me get Sam fixed up and we'll talk."

The doc was at the door when they arrived at the base hospital and after a slight struggle getting Sam untied and off the horse took both men inside.

"Take care of Sam first, Doc." Tye said stretching out on one of the beds and closing his eyes and relaxing for the first time in what seemed forever. The next thing he knew doc was removing the bandage from his head and cleansing the wound.

"How's Sam Doc?

"He'll live, but he's going to be laid up for awhile."

"Good. I was kinds worried infection might have set in."

"Might have if you hadn't used that rot gut to clean the wound."

"How did you know about that?"

"Sam came around or should I say sobered up some while I was working on him. Used some words I wouldn't want to repeat telling about your pouring good drinking whiskey on his wounds. Called you some pretty foul names too," he chuckled.

He finished with cleaning and bandaging the wound just about the time Rebecca rushed through the door and rushing into Tye's arms.

"You okay, darling?" she cried kissing him on the cheeks and lips. "You okay?"

"I'm fine, honey. Just a little scratch."

Doc laughed. "Rebecca, I've told Tye before and I've told you the same thing: that man is never going to die. I've treated him God knows how many times for different wounds and he's still here because he hasn't any vital organs, no heart, no lungs or liver, no nothing; just bone and muscle. All three laughed.

Rebecca stepped back and wrinkled her nose. "I think you need a bath and fresh clothes, honey." They laughed again.

"Where's the kids?"Tye asked as they left the hospital.

"They're with Buff at the house." She stopped suddenly. "What about Sam? I was so worried about you I forgot to ask."

He's shot up pretty good, but he'll make it. Doc gave him some stuff to make him sleep for awhile. How did you know I was here?"

"Clark is pretty big, but it's not so big that news doesn't get around pretty quick. I bet there's not a man on the fort that doesn't know you are here. I know one officer who wants' to meet you and he's making quite a name for himself here also."

"Lieutenant Bullis?" Tye asked.

Rebecca nodded. "He cuts a fine figure of a man-handsome and dashing!"

"You noticed, huh?"

"Now why would a woman notice another man when she has you?" they both snickered like two school children. "He's really looking forward to meeting you honey. He's quite impressed by what you have done for the people in this area and for the men here at the fort. I bet you there's not one thing you have done that either Sergeants Arnold, Absher, or Major Thurston hasn't told him. What they didn't tell him, Sergeant O'Malley has."

"I'd like to meet him too and also the Seminole Scouts that saved him from the Comanche awhile back."

"From what I hear from O'Malley they are really good at tracking and fighting, they don't like the Apaches, and they love Bullis."

"Let's get hom..." Tye was interrupted by a voice behind them. Stopping and turning around they saw Sergeant Absher running toward them. When he caught up with them, Tye asked. "What in hell you so excited about Sergeant?"

Absher, bent over his hands on his knees and trying to gulp in some air hesitated a few seconds before answering

"That son-of-a-bitch," then stopping looking at Rebecca tipped his hat to her and apologized for the slip of the tongue. "Tye, the man you have been chasing is at the doc's over in Bracket getting a couple of holes patched up."

Tye looked him in the eye. "How do you know this?"

"One of my men that was in the saloon heard talk that a breed came in three or so hours ago shot up and went to the doc's. I figured it was your man."

"Honey, I gotta go." He pecked her on the cheek. "See you soon." He turned to Absher. "See her home Sergeant."

"Will do Tye."

Tye was trotting away when he heard Rebecca yell, "Be careful." He waved over his shoulder and rushed across the bridge over Los Moras Creek and into Brackett and to the doc's office which was his home also. He pulled his gun as he quickly opened the door and stepped inside. He saw no one but the doc sitting in a chair and his wife who was bandaging his head. The room smelled of smoke and he saw the blackened floor and tipped over table.

"What happened Doc?" Tye asked holstering his gun.

"Don't rightly know for sure Tye."

"Well I can tell you what happened," his wife said. "My husband patched up a breed or he at least looked like one and when he was through working on the scoundrel instead of paying Doc he pistol whipped him and left."

"How long ago was this?' Tye asked.

"Maybe twenty minutes, thirty at the most," Doc's wife answered.

"You're lucky Doc." Tye said patting the old man on the shoulder.

"Lucky! How in hell can you say I was lucky? I got a damn busted head."

"I've been chasing this man and you're the only the second man he has talked to he hasn't killed." He tipped his hat to the lady and walked quickly outside. He walked across the street to where two men sat in chairs leaning back against the wall of the mercantile store.

"You men see a breed leave Doc's office a few minutes ago?"

"Shor did Tye. Left in a hurry to," one of the men answered.

"Which way did he go?"

The man doing the talking nodded his head toward the west. "Went that way, Tye."

"Thanks." Tye hurried back across the bridge then had to stop as he was out of breath and his head was spinning. Weaker than I thought, he thought to himself. Must have lost more blood than I figured too. He sat on a large rock under a pecan tree to gather himself before going to the stables to get Sandy.

A few minutes later he was saddling Sandy. He patted him on the neck. "I would like to have given you more time to recoup old boy but this here's an emergency.

"Been looking for you Tye." Tye turned to the familiar voice and saw Sergeant Absher standing there. "Major Thurston wants to see you Tye."

"It will have to wait," Tye said sharply.

Absher grabbed Sandy's reins. "He would like to see you now, Tye."

"Damn,"Tye mumbled. "Okay let's go."

Thurston was on the porch of headquarter when Tye and Absher arrived as well as four soldiers sitting on horses in front and holding the reins of a fifth horse.

"I know you are going after that man who beat the hell out of Doc so I want you to take these troopers and Sergeant Absher and go get him. I won't take no for an answer."

Tye started to argue the point but knew Thurston well enough that when his mind was made up God himself could not change it and besides, he didn't want to waste the time arguing. He looked at the troopers. "Let's ride."

Earlier, Jeb had been lying on the examining table at the doc's when a man came in with a busted nose and a torn ear. He had been in a fight at one of the saloons. Doc knew him and said he would be right with him as soon as he was through with fixing these gunshot wounds on the patient on the table. The man came over holding a bloody kerchief to his nose. The blood had dried on his neck from the cut on the ear which wasn't bad.

Doc told Jeb to lie still for a moment after he had bandaged the wounds and took the man with the busted nose into another room. As they were going through the door Jeb heard the man mention he had seen Tye Watkins and a wounded man who he thought was the other deputy, Sam Jenkins. "Looked like Tye had a head wound since he had his head wrapped." The door was then shut and all Jeb could hear was muffled voices and could not understand what was been said.

Jeb lay there thinking about what the man said. Dammit to hell, he thought. I thought I was rid of that stinking bloodhound. I should have stayed there till both were dead. Now, I got me a problem with us both in this here two-bit town. Then he had a second thought. He probably doesn't know I'm here so maybe I can get out without him ever knowing.

Doc came back into the room with the other man who thanked the doc and went through the door that led outside to the street.

"Who's this Tye Watkins fellow that man was talking about?" Jeb inquired.

Doc looked at Jeb and laughed. "Surely my good man you are joshing me. Everyone around here knows who he is."

"I ain't from around here Doc. I'm from up north a ways. Seems to me I've heard the name before, but can't rightly say where I heard it."

"Tye," the doc replied, "Is about the most famous Indian scout that ever was. Made his self more famous than his pa. He's now a lawmen and making his self known all over the State of Texas with his tracking down outlaws. Once he gets on a trail they say even a ghost would leave enough sign that Tye could follow."

Doc looked at Jeb. "Looks like you're strong enough now so you can leave if you have a mind to. I wouldn't do anything strenuous that might reopen those wounds." He held out his hand to Jeb. "That's five dollars for fixing you up young man."

Jeb slid off the table and pretended as if he was reaching into his pocket, but instead he pulled his gun and struck the old man on the side of the head. Doc never uttered a word, but as he fell to the floor he knocked over a table with a lighted lamp on it which came crashing to the floor spilling the kerosene which caught fire.

Jeb walked outside as casually as he could and forked his horse and started walking the horse down the street. He hadn't gone but half a block when he heard someone holler fire. He nudged his horse into a trot and left town on the Old Mail Road headed west toward Mexico. He knew one thing for certain; Watkins would be after him damn quick.

He wasn't going straight to the border since he was a hot item on the most wanted list that every damn Mexican officer had in his pocket. He would travel north and west following the Rio Bravo (Rio Grande) River for a hundred or so miles then cross into Mexico where the troops and

Federales would not be so many. He knew he didn't have enough supplies but that was no problem for a man like himself-*there was always stupid gringos living far from neighbors he could kill and take what he needed,* he thought to himself. He smiled at the thought and then grimaced as pain shot thru his leg reminding him again why he wanted to kill the gringo, Watkins and that other deputy.

Tye and the soldiers had their horses at an easy canter on the Old Mail Road. He had Absher and three of the troopers on the left side and himself and one trooper on the right or north side. They were watching for fresh tracks leaving the road. Jeb was in Tye's head and like he always did he was trying to figure out what the man he was chasing had in mind, what he figured to do. Most of the time he was successful in doing this and managed to stay with a man even though he might have lost his tracks. *I figure he's going north and maybe not into Mexico since it's pretty warm over them for him with everyone looking for him.*

Ten miles from town Absher reined in and pointed to the ground where fresh tracks left the road. Tye dismounted and keeling down studied the tracks.

"This isn't his tracks Sergeant."

"How can you tell Tye?" One of the privates asked.

Tye answered after stepping into the Saddle. "No two horses have the same tracks son, just as men don't. I've been following this horse for a spell now and I know his tracks like

I know the back of my hand." He reined Sandy back to other side of the road.

"Good job Absher, just keep an eye out for more tracks."

Five miles father Tye reined in Sandy and dismounted to study some tracks. After kneeling and studying he stood up and patted Sandy on the neck with one hand and scratched him on the forehead with the other while studying the lay of the land where the tracks were headed.

"Those the tracks?" Absher asked.

Tye turned toward the men and nodded. "I don't know if the Sergeant here or Major Thurston spoke to you about the man we are chasing or not." He looked at the men's faces, really looked for the first time and thought- *Hell, they ain't a one of them over twenty years old except the sergeant.* "Let me fill you in on just what we are facing. No telling how many men, women, horses, dogs' cats, and whatever else this man has killed. He is a killing machine, a man so full of hate that there is no room for a conscious or mercy. He was done a wrong by men killing his family and then later men massacred the tribe he was living with. One of you, maybe two of you or hell, maybe all of us ain't gonna make it back to Clark. That is how dangerous this man is. As long as he breathes he will seek vengeance. By the looks of the tracks we are less than an hour behind him so ride easy, alert and be ready for anything. Let's go."

Chapter 11

An hour later, Tye halted the little group and dismounted. He kneeled down on one knee and traced the track with his finger. "His horse has thrown a shoe. Things will get real interesting from here on." He mounted Sandy, slid his Henry out of its leather and nudged Sandy forward at a slow walk.

"Damn!" Absher exclaimed. "I hate it when he says that."

"Watcha mean by that Sergeant?" Private Benton asked.

Absher took out a plug and bit off a bite and chewed on it for a moment before answering. "It means son that things are going to get real hot and damn quick as in bullets flying and men dying. That's what it means. Now ya'll shuck those rifles out and keep them handy and watch for trouble. If you see Tye leap off Sandy and hit the ground I suggest you be right behind him and hit it also." They followed Tye a few paces behind Sandy.

Jeb, a mile or so ahead, was cursing his luck. His horse was limping badly and he was now walking, leading the crippled horse looking for a place to hole up. For the second time lately he felt a little bit of fear. It wasn't a fear of dying, but a fear of not accomplishing what he wanted most and that was killing more whites and Mexicans who he hated even more than the whites. *Well that last thought was true about the Mexicans,* he thought to himself, *but there is one white man I hate above all and he was probably on his trail right now and not too far behind.*

He spotted a small cave on the rim of the canyon that looked like it would serve his purpose as far as a place to hole up and had a good field of fire. *I will try to fool this scout one more time*, he thought as he moved to the side of his horse and mounted and walked him slowly down the canyon. The cave he had spotted was still about a hundred yards from him and he studied the lay of the land as he approached it and liking what he saw." If this is the end of the trail for me this is a good spot to die," he mumbled to himself knowing he had a good chance to kill more white eyes from there.

When he was almost below the cave he halted his limping horse and stepped carefully from the saddle to a large rock. He took his saddle bags, his canteen and the

Henry from its sheath and slapped the horse across the hindquarters with the barrel. The startle horse leaped a few feet and limped quickly on down the trail. *If I'm still alive after this I can get Watkins horse and go on.* He carefully, as only an Apache could, made his way up the slope angling toward the cave. Reaching the place he had chosen he was surprised how deep it was. *That's a good thing*, he thought. *At least there won't be any ricochets hitting me in the back.*

He stepped over the ledge in front of the opening and immediately froze. He had almost jumped on the top of a rattler that must be five foot long and as big around as his upper arm. The snake was in the well know S position, his head back and his tongue going in and out rapidly, ready to strike. The buzz from it rattlers was extremely loud in the confined space. His only alternative was to draw his pistol and kill it. He chanced a quick look at the trail he had come on. He could see a mile or so down it and saw no one. He turned back, aimed and fired his pistol. The snakes head disappeared in red spray and watched as its body writhed on the rocky floor. He quickly looked around and saw no more. He took the barrel of his Henry and flipped the snake to the far side of the cave knowing if need be the snake would be a tasty meal.

He was on the east rim of the canyon and it was a little higher than the west rim. Looking west over the rim Jeb could see the high mountains in Mexico that had been his and his people's home for generations. At least it was his family's people's home. He had not ever felt he was completely accepted by the Apache and he had seen firsthand how the Mex and whites treated breeds. Still he wished he was in those mountains. He had always loved the smell of dust free air and the smell of the cedars, sage, and the few pines that grew there. There were a few springs that had clear cold water and trout that the white in him loved. For the most part, Apaches shunned fish as far as eating them. Jeb wiped those thoughts away as he settled back and watched his back trail.

Tye reined Sandy in and sat there taking in the lay of the land n front of him.

"Something wrong Tye?" Absher asked.

"Hear what sounded like a shot up ahead, but can't say for certain," Tye answered. He sat there for a moment longer listening. The slight breeze was in his face and he knew would have carried the sound a long ways. It could have been a mile or it could have been farther. Regardless he was sure it had been a shot he heard and probably from a pistol.

"Ride easy like," he said to the others.

As they rode the only sound was the creaking of leather, hooves striking a stone and the occasional cough of one of the men. Absher wiped the sweat from his face with his kerchief and then tied it back around his neck. He watched the hills, but he also watched the man in front of him, Tye. Tye's head never moved but Absher knew his eyes were scanning every nook and cranny looking for trouble. He knew he was looking for ambush sites and no one was better at spotting them than that man riding in front of him. He thought back to his days on patrols when Tye was scouting. Me and every man at Clark felt comfortable on patrol with Tye. Sure as hell didn't with the other scouts accept maybe for Dan. Dan was good, having been taught personally by Tye, but still he wasn't Tye and that uncomfortable feeling, maybe a little fear, was always there where it wasn't with Tye out front. Sure we were feared of the Apache and knew there was a good chance of dying, but you just felt like it wasn't going to happen when Tye was there. It was a sad day for the troops when Tye gave up scouting and started being a lawman. Tye held up his hand and the little troop held up. Tye dismounted and studied the tracks on the ground for a moment. He stood up and looked in the direction the tracks went before turning to the men.

"This is fixing to end pretty damn quick men," he said. "His horse can no longer carry him so Jed is on foot leading his horse. He may hole up and try to kill more of us white eyes or he may light a shuck for Mexico."

"The Border is fifteen mile or so away," one of the trooper said.

Tye looked at the man. "Don't forget he's half Apache and an Apache can cover fifty or more miles a day on foot if he has to."

An astonished look appeared on the troopers face. "Fifty miles?"

"More than that if need be," Tye replied.

"Hell, son," Absher replied. "I know this man here," nodding toward Tye, "saved my ass and a lot of troopers one time up where the Rio Grande and the Rio Brazos run together by running forty miles in the dark to get us a relief patrol back when we was pinned down by a hundred or so Apaches. If he can do it believe what he says when he tells you it would be no problem for an Apache."

"Have your men ride careful like with their boots out of the stirrups so they can get off in a hurry," Tye said looking at Absher.

"You heard what the man said," the sergeant said. "Do it."

Tye remounted and continued up the trail even more alert now than before for the puff of smoke from a rifle or a glimpse of something reflecting the sun-anything that would give him just an instant warning.

After about twenty minutes of gut wrenching pressure of expecting a bullet any second Tye spotted the cave on the rim ahead of him maybe a quarter of a mile away. Glad he doesn't have a big Sharps Fifty or one of us would be dead right now, he mused. He dismounted and indicated for the others to also. He nodded to the cave on the left rim of the canyon.

"His horse is in a bad way so I figure he's going to try and get another one," Tye said.

"Been out here before several times on patrol," a young private named Benson said. "Don't recall no homestead or ranches around here where he can get one."

"Are you riding a horse?" Absher asked.

"I sure ain't walking Sarge. What does that have to do with…"

"He needs a horse private," Absher interrupted. "I have one, you have one."

"Still I…" then he paused when he thought about it. "Yeah, I see what you mean." He looked at the rim where the cave was and walked around on the other side of his horse-the side away from the cave.

Tye checked the position of the sun. "Be getting dark pretty soon. We'll make camp over there," he said nodding to a group of large boulders. They will offer some protection and the loose stones on the ground all around will make it difficult for anyone to get into camp without us hearing him."

When the horses were picketed and cared for Absher told Benson and Hughes to get a small fire started and coffee on. Use dead wood for the fire."

Private Hughes asked. "Sarge, shouldn't we just make a dry camp and not advertise where we are with a fire."

El Diablo

Tye was listening and smiled when Absher replied. "Hell private, don't you think that son-of-a-bitch knows we are back here following him especially if he's up there in that cave watching and waiting to blow some privates dumbass head off. Now get the damn coffee made pronto."

"Ye…Yes Sir Sarge. Will do."

Absher turned and saw Tye smiling at him and he smiled back, shook his head and walked over to where Tye sat on a large rock and sat down beside him.

Absher chuckled. "Never saw so many troopers now so wet behind the ears and so damn young. I bet Hughes there ain't eighteen years old."

Tye nodded watching the young troopers as they scurried about setting up camp. "They are getting younger and greener, but then I've know a lot of them that didn't know which end of a gun the bullet come out that's made great soldiers." He put his hand on Absher's shoulder."Seems like I heard some stories about a young private named Absher a few years back that knew how to fight with his fist and use a gun but little else and he's turned out just fine." He laughed.

Absher laughed too. "I guess you are right about that Tye. I was about as green as they come as far as being a soldier and not caring too much about following orders. I wish I had a dollar for every day I spent in the guardhouse those first two or so years before I become a 'top soldier' he said with emphasis on the top and laughed.

Tye nodded. "You've done right well Sarge. I always wanted you, Christian, and Garner on patrol with me."

"I miss Christian every day Tye. He was a good friend and one hell of a soldier. I hadn't shed a tear for years, but when I found him lying there with all those dead Apaches around him I just couldn't hold them back."

Tye patted him on the back. "Did I tell you I met his pa a few days ago?"

Absher's head rose quickly. "You're joshing me. You met his pa?"

"Yeah. Sam and me were following Jeb and found where he had killed a couple men in a town and I was questioning some of the townspeople and this man asked me if I was the Watkins that scouted at Clark. Told me his son was a trooper there before he got his self killed by Apaches. When he told me his name I couldn't believe it. I promised him I would come back and visit him and his wife."

"I sure would like to go with you Tye. I've got time off coming. Maybe I can swing it."

"Glad to have you along when I go, but right now we've got to deal with this guy that I think is watching us from that cave waiting for the chance to kill one of us.

El Diablo

Chapter Twelve

"How we going to handle it?" Absher asked while looking at the cave. "This situation reminds me of a while back when I was with you and we had that outlaw Mills trapped in a cave like this."

"We'll handle it the same way we did that time." Tye answered. "Ya'll watch the cave and if you can get a little closer without exposing yourself go ahead. I'll see if I can get around back of him and box him in." Absher nodded his understanding and Tye left on foot, backtracking before leaving the trail to begin working his way behind where he figured Jeb was.

Ten minutes later, Tye heard the crack of a rifle and knew the soldiers had been spotted. *That was a Henry, not a Spencer that Absher and the others carried*, he thought to himself.

The back of Charlie Howe's head exploded as the slug from the Henry entered his forehead and exited in the rear of his skull. Blood, bone fragments and gore splattered in the face of the soldier behind him, a young man by the name of Larry Houser. Larry, frozen to the spot, stared at his dead friend's body which lay crumpled on the ground in front of him.

"Keep your damn heads down," Absher ordered as he looked at Howe lying in the dirt. He had seen many a trooper down and was a little more calloused than the other men who had not saw much action as of yet and never one of their buddies killed, but it still bothered him. He could cover the feeling up somewhat after all these years, but it still hurt to see a fellow trooper die like that especially one so young with his whole life ahead of him. "Stay down and follow me."

"Sarge, what about Charlie?" Private Houser asked. "We just going to leave him lying there all bloody?" He asked, his voice almost breaking.

"He's beyond help Houser," Absher said. "Unless you want to join him I suggest you pull yourself together and do what I say or I'll shoot you myself." he added in a threatening voice. Absher's head snapped around quickly and looked up the slope as several shots were fired in rapid succession. He quickly knew they were from behind the hill and guessed Jeb had made a break for it and ran into Tye.

"Private Baines!" the sergeant almost shouting his name.

"Yes Sir."

"You stay here and don't leave this post till I get back. Anything or anyone comes down that hill without hollering your name, shoot. Do you understand?"

"H..How long do I wait Sarge?" A nervous private asked.

"I just told you, Private Baines. You stay at this spot till me or Tye comes and gets you."

"Yes Sir. "

Absher turned to Houser. "Let's go see if Tye's okay."

A few minutes earlier Jeb had all the men spotted- all in blue coats and he knew what that meant. No Watkins with them so he must be trying to circle and come in behind him. He took a quick look back at the soldiers and none were looking up at him right now so he leapt back over the rocky ledge in front of the cave and scrambled over the rim of the canyon dropping to the ground immediately. He scooted on his belly a couple feet to his right and snuggled in behind a fairly thick cedar. He took his hat off and laid it beside him and using the barrel of his Henry moved the branches slightly apart so he could try and spot Watkins.

He caught a movement out of the corner of his eye to his left and moved the barrel slightly in that direction and prepared himself to shoot the famous scout.

Tye thought he had caught a glimpse of Jeb as he came over the crest of the canyon, but it was only for an instant as the man dropped out of sight. Tye was fifty yards in front of where he had seen Jeb and was slightly below him. He stayed where he was crouched behind a large boulder and waited. Tye figured as quick as Jeb came over the edge he doubted the man had time to scan the area and doubted he had saw him. But one could bet his last dollar he was watching now.

Tye saw another boulder with a couple thick cedars. Let's find out if he's watching or not. Tye sprinted toward the other boulder which was only four or five good strides away. He ran in a crouch and was glad he did because a bullet cut the air about where he head would have been and that bullet was followed by two more which were fired so fast they almost sounded as one. He reached the boulder and cedars and quickly brought his Henry up and fired three times as fast as he could lever shells into the chamber at the cedar where the smoke from the shots fired by Jeb still drifted in the air around the cedar.

Tye knew it would have been a lucky shot if one of the ones he fired had actually connected with Jeb and he wasn't one to depend much on luck. He would play the Apache game of patience and wait awhile. He reached behind and took out three shells from his belt and without taking his eyes off where Jeb was hidden fed them into his Henry. He was staring at the cedar when he detected a slight movement in the limbs and suddenly realized what he was looking at was the barrel of a rifle. He ducked his head and an instant later a bullet whistled by where his head had been.

Tye shook his head and muttered to himself. "That was close-way to close." Then he thought. *I've got to get to a better place to watch from. Looks to me like with me being below him he could scoot to his right or left and get plum away without me seeing him do so if he stayed low.* He had a lot of respect for the man's fighting ability and smarts as far as being a hard man to trap, but now he had all new respect. *What senses he has can't be taught*, Tye thought. *He's good and along with being as smart and cagey as he is he's hell on wheels with that rifle. I've tracked a lot of Apaches and some other bad hombres that were cagey, but I believe this one is the best.* He then mumbled to himself, "And definitely the most dangerous." As good as he is with that Henry Tye figured the shot he heard earlier had ended one of the trooper's lives on this here earth. He pondered on that for a moment. *If one of them was hit and I hope they hadn't I pray it wasn't Absher. He could keep them in line and would know what to do. If he was hit no telling what those green recruits would do.* He waited and as he watched the rim he also looked for a spot to move to that would give him a better position to see things. He waited.

Nothing moved. It was quieter than a meeting house just before the preacher started delivering his words praising the Lord and damning the sinners. He glanced up and didn't even see a buzzard which was rare in this country. No sound, not even any birds chirping. He waited some more.

Jeb replaced the spent rounds in the Henry and sat there contemplating his next move. *I need to get across the river into Mexico, but I need a horse which it don't look like I'm gonna get without a good chance of getting shot. Them bluecoats will be coming up behind me and with that damn scout down there in front it don't leave me much choice.* He crawled fifteen feet to his right where he found a game trail that led farther to the right and around the hill. He followed the trail keeping his head below the tops of the sage, cactus, and cedars. Once he was around the side of the hill he pointed his boots west and started the ground eating trot of the Apache glancing over his shoulder every minute or so watching for any sign of Watkins or the soldiers.

Tye waited five more minutes and saw no movement and heard no sound. Just as he started to move he saw a flash of blue on the ridge and he froze. He relaxed when he heard the familiar voice of Absher.

"You okay Tye?"

Since the voice was coming from where he figured Jeb was, he knew the man was gone. *Damn him to hell*, he thought.

"Down here Sarge," he shouted back and stood up.

The soldiers saw him and headed down the slope toward him.

El Diablo

Tye stopped them. "Absher, you and your men go back to where the horses are and circle back of this hill. I'll meet you at the bottom.

"Yo," Absher replied and Tye watched them as they went back over the rim and disappear. He climbed up to the place where he had seen Jeb. He found the spent cartridges and the tracks following the game trail. He quickly followed them to where he saw the foot prints leaving the trail and heading west. *It's going to be a race to the Border now for sure*. He studied the lay of the land in that direction. He knew exactly what the terrain was like between here and the Border having been over it many a time chasing Apache. *Our horses are not going to be much of an advantage*, he thought, *not with all the steep hills, wash outs, thick stands of mesquite, cactus, and cedars*. He remember the last time he was in this area chasing the Apache war chief, Grey Owl and remembering the only thing that saved him from being killed was that the Apache had not cocked his Spencer before getting into position behind Tye for the killing shot. Tye had moved at the metallic click of the rifle being cocked and the bullet just nicked him in the shoulder. Tye shuddered at the thought of how close that had been.

He backtracked to where Jeb had been and headed downhill to where he had left Sandy. The soldiers arrived there at the same time as he did. Tye winced when he saw the blue clad figure lying across the saddle of one of the mounts.

"Where is that bastard?" Absher asked.

"He's headed toward Mexico," Tye replied.

"He thinks he can out run these horses?" Private Baines questioned not believing the man could think that.

"He's pretty damn sure he can and I'm not so sure he's not right."

"B..but how can he expect…"

"The terrain, Private," Tye said cutting him off. "There are hills too steep for a horse to go up or down, there's arroyos, think stands of mesquite, cactus and cedars. Everything that slows a horse down is there plus he knows we will be moving cautious because there are a million places a man can hide and pick a man off with an easy shot." Tye paused and mounted Sandy. "I'd say he has a damn good chance and there's a good possibility not all of us will make it back so if I was you I'd stay alert and keep my eyes peeled for trouble and maybe, just maybe you won't be one of those that don't. He's already killed one good trooper. He turned his head a little and gave Absher a wink.

Absher turned his head away from the men and smiled. *Tye has a way with words that will keep a man from getting too comfortable.* He chuckled to himself.

"Can either of you men find your way back to the fort," Tye asked looking at Baines and House. The two men looked at each other, neither saying anything. Tye didn't figure they could and it wasn't unusual. Troopers for the most part, with the exception of most officers and non-coms, paid little attention where they were when on patrol. They spent most of their time daydreaming about getting back and downing a few beers or going to battle with some of the girls in the rooms above the saloons.

"Wrap the private there in his blanket and secure the ends tight with rope. Then wrap his slicker tight around the blanket and secured the ends of it tight. It may be a couple days till we can get him back to the fort for proper burial," Tye said.

Five minutes later they were on their way headed into what Tye knew would be a miserable and very dangerous fifteen or so miles to the Border.

Chapter Thirteen

Four hours of skirting washes, deep arroyos, thick stands of mesquite and cedars and steep hills and everything else this country could throw at a man to slow him down found four men staring at the set of foot prints leading into the shallow waters of the Rio Grande River that was the Border between Texas and Mexico.

Tye sat on Sandy staring across the river to where the tracks came out on the other side.

"What we gonna do now, Tye?" Absher questioned.

"I'm studying on it," Tye answered. "Give me a minute." The three soldiers sat on their mounts waiting instructions. Tye reined Sandy around and faced the men.

"You men can go back to Clark. It's a day and a half ride. We need to pool our food and see what we have."

"Are you thinking what I think you are?" Absher asked.

"Probably," Tye replied. He took off his U.S. Marshal's badge and handed it to Absher. "Give this to Rebecca and I'll get it when I get back."

"I knew you couldn't let that damn breed go. You know what you are in for over there better than we do so you be damn careful. I don't want to see Rebecca have to get the news of your demise."

"What's demise mean, Sarge?" House asked.

Absher stared at the private. "Killed, dead, passed on, you idiot."

"Oh," the private said obviously embarrassed."

Tye put his hand on the private's shoulder. "Don't fret any. I wasn't sure what it meant either," he lied and winked at Absher and Baines.

They dismounted and combining their food and laying it on a flat rock. It wasn't much. Some jerky and a few biscuits, a half pound of bacon and some coffee lay on the rock. Tye took a little of the jerky, four biscuits, and sliced a little bacon from the slab for himself.

"I figure what left there should keep you three from starving till you get back to the fort."

There were eight biscuits left. Absher picked two of them up and handed them to Tye. "Take these. You don't know how long it will be before you get back. You may need'um."

Tye nodded and put them with the other food in his saddle bag and wishing the Spencer's that the soldiers had used the same caliber of bullet his Henry did. Absher was thinking the same thing. He handed Tye his Spencer and taking some of the .56 caliber shells from the two privates handed Tye about forty rounds. "You may need these before you make it back. Just make sure you make it back with my Spencer. I don't want the damn army deducting the cost from my paycheck," he chuckled.

"That'd be just like the army," Tye answered laughing. "When you get back to the fort tell Rebecca I'll see her in a few days."

Absher leaned to his right in the saddle and shook Tye's hand. "I'll tell her, Tye. You take care of yourself." He reined his mount around and led the soldiers away. Tye watched the men ride off headed north toward Clark. He leaned forward and patted Sandy on the neck.

"Well ole boy, we're alone again." Sandy nickered and shook his head. Tye smiled and nudged Sandy into the shallow waters of the Rio Grande and crossed into Mexico.

Jeb was tired, bone tired. He had been walking or trotting for hours and he was more than ready to find a mount he could steal. He was headed south staying within a quarter mile or so of the river. He was looking for a ranch or even a single home, any place that might have a horse. Thirty minutes later he came upon a Mexican vaquero herding a small bunch of longhorns that probably had been taken from a ranch across the river in Texas. At this time in Texas history it was common knowledge that a lot of ranchers on both sides of the Border would 'borrow' a few head of cattle from the neighbors across the river.

The vaquero had not spotted him so he stayed in the brush and worked his was closer coming up to the man from behind. When he was twenty feet from the man the vaquero reined his mount in and began rolling a smoke. Jeb smiled.

He moved to within fifteen feet of the unsuspecting man and not wanting to alert anyone that might be around by firing his pistol he removed his Bowie and holding the point between his thumb and index finger deftly threw the knife toward the back of the man. The knife spun one time and struck the man dead center of the back between the shoulder blades burying itself to the hilt and penetrating the man's heart. The man grunted and leaned forward in the saddle and then slid slowly to the ground. He twitched a couple times and then lay still.

Jeb pulled the knife out of the man's back, wiped it on the man's pants and stuck it back in the beaded sheath on his belt. He looked around for anyone that might have seen what happened and seeing no one, mounted the horse and continued south feeling much better about things.

Four miles down the trail he pulled up suddenly as he spotted a lone rider about three quarters of a mile in front of him. "Damn!" he cursed, when he spotted the uniformed men a hundred or so yards behind the lone rider. "Scout for the Federales," he mumbled to himself as he jerked the reins and led his mount off the trail toward the river. He knew the scout would see his tracks and follow him so he rode into the river and crossed back into Texas knowing they would not follow across the border.

He walked his horse behind a stand of mesquite and dismounted and lay on his belly watching the far bank. The scout showed up about fifteen minutes later and as Jeb watched, he stepped from the saddle and kneeled on the bank looking at the tracks. After a few seconds he stood up and looked across the river directly where Jeb laid hidden deep in the shadows of the thick mesquite. Jeb knew the scout could not see him unless he moved.

"Damn," he mumbled as ants were crawling on his hands and shirt and some were now on his neck and inside of his shirt. He didn't dare move for any movement would give him away and though the Federales would not cross the river their bullets could. Jeb knew they were as ruthless as the banditos and the Apache they chased and would no doubt not pass up a chance to kill what they figured was a gringo who had no business being in their country in the first place.

A minute passed with the ants stinging, gnats buzzing around his face and Jeb not moving. It was great relief when he saw the scout mount back up and disappear into the brush and trees. He stood up and slapped at the ants on his hands and face then removed his shirt and wiped the rest off. He figured he had been stung about twenty or so times and would be a little painful for short time and then probably itch for a while, but no more than a minor discomfort.

He mounted his horse and sat there rolling himself a smoke and contemplating on things. He was back in Texas where he did not want to be so he thought about his next step. He knew a little farther south was a fairly large town named Eagle Pass. *Maybe I could ride there and hole up for a few days. Watkins does not know what I look like other than maybe a vague description given to him. I can clean up, cut my hair and maybe lose him there. Last I heard there were a lot of people living there.* He smiled at his next thought. *Hell, I may get close enough to him to use my knife.* He got a little excited at the thought of plunging a blade into the scout. A knife was just so much more personal than a bullet and always gave him a satisfied feeling. He headed south.

Tye was kneeling over the dead vaquero when Sandy snorted. Tye stood up quickly and looked in the direction Sandy was looking. He cursed under his breath.

"Damn Federales." He cursed because he knew he was in trouble what with him being a white man standing over a dead Mexican. He had a choice to make and damn quick; stand and try and talk his way out of this situation or run like hell for the river and Texas. *Ain't much for running, but I'm betting they don't speak English so my trying to explain anything would do no good.* He leaped in the saddle not bothering with the stirrups and reined Sandy east, toward the Rio Grande. Sandy could run like no other horse he had ever owned. He glanced back and saw four or five men chasing him while the rest were around the dead vaquero. The men chasing him were about two hundred yards behind him when he felt a tug on his left sleeve and then heard the boom of a rifle and glanced back.

He cursed under his breath again when he saw the men had halted and one was bringing up a rifle again. *Damn Sharps.* He reined Sandy to the left just as he heard the bullet cutting the air where he had been and then the boom of the heavy rifle again. He was almost three hundred yards from them now and felt a little better but he knew the range of the old buffalo gun was almost a mile and the man using it was good. He reined Sandy left and then right and left again and then instead of back to the right he went left again not wanting the man to get a pattern on his movements. He glanced over his shoulder and saw the man with the rifle mounting his horse and all of them headed his direction running dead out. He leaned over the Saddle and patted Sandy on the neck.

"Run ole boy, run." As if Sandy understood the situation he picked up a little more speed and a few seconds later Tye saw the river and let out a sigh of relief. Then he saw the Apaches.

Chapter Fourteen

The Apaches had him cut off from the river so he reined Sandy into an arroyo and jumped from the saddle grabbing his Henry and prepared to make a stand. He slapped Sandy on the rump to get him to move a little farther out of the line of fire. He saw the Apaches, about fifteen in number coming from his right and the five Federales coming from his left. Apparently the Federales had not spotted the Apaches as of yet for they were coming fast.

Tye glanced back to his right and was surprised to see no Apaches, but knowing them like he did he wasn't surprised. *They aren't going to risk losing anyone on a frontal assault so they will be coming from two or three directions on foot*, he figured. He was trapped and knew he was in big time trouble. He was hopping mad at himself for letting himself get caught in this situation. *Well, if I'm going down I'm gonna bring hellfire and brimstone on the ones trying to kill me.* He checked his Henry and his Colt to make sure they were fully loaded and took a handful of cartridges and lay then on a rock close by so they would be handy. He could see the Federales well now as they were less than a hundred yards away. They had slowed their mounts to a trot and the man in front was looking at Tye's tracks.

Tye watched as the man in front raised his hand and all stopped. He looked at the ground and then to where the tracks led and saw Tye in the rocks. He spread the men out in a crude skirmish line and when he yelled something in Spanish they all kicked their horses into an all out run toward Tye. Tye took aim on the man in the middle of the pack and slowly squeezed the trigger, but before the Henry fired he heard an eruption of rifle fire and three of the men were blown off their mounts. A fourth man was laying across his saddle and barely staying in it as the fifth man had the injured man's reins and was racing away when a volley of shots swept both men from their saddles.

Five men were down and probably dead in less than ten seconds. Tye sat there and waited for the end to come. He could not help but admire the Apaches even though he knew he could not survive fifteen of them trying to kill him. They had set up that ambush on the fly, not having time to plan it out. He shook his head at the ability of these fighting men. He waited for the rush of warriors.

El Diablo

Five minutes went by and nothing happened. Then of a sudden he heard a voice speaking in broken English.

"Waa-kins." Then again louder, "Waa-kins." *What the heck is going on?* Tye wondered.

"I'm here," he shouted and as he did so an Apache appeared about sixty yards in front of him.

"Wa-kins" the Apache repeated and then said the magic word. "Yahzie, Yahzie."

"I be damned," Tye mumbled and stood up. By now the Apache was close enough for him to recognize his friend and climbed out of the arroyo and walked toward him, the Henry in his right hand pointed toward the ground but his finger was on the trigger just in case.

As they came together Tye asked. "What is my friend Yahzie doing this far south?"

"Following my friend," Yahzie replied in broken English. "We see you cross river into Mexico and follow to see what you do. Why you here?"

The other Apaches came from hiding and walked up to where Yahzie and Tye were standing which made the ex-scout a little nervous, but they were relaxed and carrying their rifles loosely at their sides. He answered Yahzie. "Do you know the breed called El Diablo?"

Yahzie nodded. "Man who kills Mexicans and whites. Friend of Apache. Why you ask Yahzie about El Diablo?"

After hearing the remark "friend to Apache" Tye knew he had better watch what he said so he told a little white lie. "For no reason he shot my friend," then took his hat off and pointed to the bullet burn on the side of his head, "and almost killed me for no reason. I want to catch him and find out why he did this thing."

Yahzie nodded. "El Diablo needs no reason. He hates all who not Apache. You kill him?"

Tye shook his head. "Not unless he forces me to," which was not a lie. He then added. "Tye thanks his friend for saving him from Federales."

Yahzie smiled. "Yahzie thinks Waa-kins no need help but we kill Mexicans anyway."

Tye smiled. "There are fifteen or more Mexican soldiers near and will be here soon," he said knowing the Apache probably already knew this.

Yahzie nodded. "The man you look for cross river back into Texas and rode his pony south.

"You saw this?

Yahzie nodded toward a tall, muscular warrior. "He follows man known as El Diablo and watched him cross back into Texas to avoid the Mexican soldiers."

El Diablo

This did not surprise Tye. The Apache always seemed to know everything that was going on around wherever they were. He placed his hand on Yahzie's shoulder. "I must go now. It has been good to see my friend again and I thank you again for helping me."

Yahzie nodded and turned with the others and trotted off to wherever their ponies were. Tye watched them for a minute then mounted Sandy and headed south along the bank of the river looking for fresh tracks and pondering over where Jeb might go. *The only town I know of close is Eagle Pass, but if he goes there he had better be on his best behavior because of the sheriff.* Tye had never met the man who ruled Eagle Pass. He had heard stories about the man from some of the soldiers at Clark who had been stationed at Fort Duncan and from a couple outlaws who he had captured who had run encounters with Sheriff J.A. Hruska. He was reportedly a big man who was no stranger when it came to using his fist, was quick on the draw and didn't hesitate to shoot if need be. He was also honest as the day is long and ran a clean town. *He has to be quite a man to run the town whose population had to be eighty or so per cent Mexican,* Tye figured. He then chuckled as a thought came to him. *If Jeb is going to Eagle Pass he's jumping out of the frying pan into the fire with Hruska there as sheriff and me on his tail. If Hruska is like most good sheriffs I know he will know if a stranger comes into town even a town with several hundred people living there like Eagle Pass.*

Twenty minutes later he found the tracks coming from the river. Kneeling, he studied them closely. It was the same tracks of the horse where the vaquero was killed. Most men out here paid attention to the horse a man rides as to color, markings etc. He also knows every horse has a different way of walking or if he is tracking a horse maybe a crack in a shoe or maybe the horse has a limp or a hoof that turns in or out just a little. All men out here pay attention to color of a horse and the brand but men like Tye also paid attention to the track and could follow it even through a mess of other tracks.

Tye followed the tracks for over an hour before he was sure Eagle Pass was Jeb's destination. He then forgot about the tracks and nudged Sandy into an easy, mile eating gallop.

A few miles outside of Eagle Pass Jeb came upon a teenage Mexican boy that was herding a small flock of sheep. He was about the same height and build as Jeb which was bad luck for the youngster. Jeb left the body in some brush after taking his pants, shirt, sandals, and sombrero. He put the clothes on after putting his in one of his saddle bags. He would hide his horse just outside of town and go in on foot like all the other peasant men did. A poor Mexican sheep herder on a horse as fine as the one he was riding would stick out like a sore thumb and for once, he didn't want attention.

After placing his Colt and knife in his pants with the baggy white shirt covering them he walked into town and headed for the nearest saloon. It took his eyes a few seconds to adjust from the bright sunlight to the dimness of the room, but when it did he saw a large man standing at the bar looking at him. He had a badge on his chest.

Tye saw the three buzzards circling and reined Sandy off the poor excuse for a road into the brush. He saw the sheep milling around nibbling at anything that grew out of the ground. He rode around the flock his eyes searching for the man herding the sheep because he knew a man never left his flock alone not with the coyotes, wolves, and big cats around. A minute later he felt disgusted. He could see a body behind some brush and dismounting he hurried over to where the body lay.

"Damn," he cursed. "This is a kid no more than fifteen or sixteen years old. The side of his head was caved in probably by the barrel of Jeb's Colt." He stood up and looked around. He figured out Jeb had changed clothes and from the tracks leading to where his horse was left wore sandals instead of boots. *Going to blend in with the Mexican population of Eagle Pass*, he thought, *and I don't have a clue what he looks like other than his size and that's not going to help since he's the same size as ninety percent of the other Mexicans. My only hope is Hruska. He may recognize him as a stranger.*

Jeb walked up to the bar and took off his sombrero and placed it on the counter top. He was aware of the eyes of the man with the badge was burning a hole through him.

He's probably trying to place me to see if my face matches any wanted posters he may have, Jeb figured.

"Hey, you," the man said rather loudly.

Jeb looked around and then pointed to his chest and in his best Spanish and his most innocent manner of speaking answered. "You speak to me?"

"Do I look like I'm talking to myself?"

"No, but why do you speak to me. I only arrived in this town a little while ago and not know you."

"That's why I'm talking to you. Didn't think I recognized you. Why are you here?"

Jeb took up his sombrero off the bar and held it in front of him turning the brim in his hands as if he was scared. "Ju…jusr passing through. I thought I might get a shot of tequila before I continued my journey."

"And where are you heading?"

"To see my mother who lives about thirty miles farther south of Eagle Pass."

"What's your name?

"Pablo, Mr. Sheriff. Pablo Guerra.

"You don't look Mex to me Pablo. Look more like a breed."

Jeb was getting fed up with this nosey sheriff, but kept his cool. "My mother is Mexican; my father was a full blood Apache."

"You said was?"

"My father was killed when I was but a small boy by the soldiers of Fort Duncan."

Hruska stared hard at the man for a log moment. "Go ahead and have your drink, but I will be watching you so you'd better be on your best behavior." Hruska turned and bellied up to the bar and downed the shot of whiskey that was there when the conversation ended.

Jeb took his glass and walked over to a table and sat down, his back to the wall. A man at the table next to him spoke.

"Watch yourself around the sheriff. He's meaner than a rattler when he gets his back up. He's a fair man though and a good sheriff. This town needed him when he came here three years ago. It's a nice place to live now and he's the one responsible."

Jed downed his tequila. "Nosey as hell if you ask me."

"Maybe, but he does that to all strangers, ask questions I mean. He wants to know everyone and is just curious when a stranger comes by. He's caught more than one man that was on the dodge by being as you say, nosey. He's planted a few in boot hill too. He's one tough son-of-a-bitch when he has to be. Just don't rile him while you are here and you won't have a problem."

"Sounds like good advice friend. Thanks." He held up his empty glass when the bartender was looking and another drink was poured. He decided to just sit, watch and listen.

Sheriff Hruska finished his drink, glanced over at Jeb then walked out of the saloon and walked to his office. *Something about that breed that's familiar*, he thought as he sat down in his chair and picked up a stack of posters. He was half through the stack when his door opened and a man as big as himself walked in. *He's as tall as me but in a hell of a lot better shape*, he thought as he stood up to shake the man's extended hand.

"Sheriff Hruska," he said shaking the man's hand.

"Deputy U.S. Marshal Tye Watkins," Tye said releasing the hand of Hruska. "I need to talk to you."

Hruska, like just about everyone else had heard of this man and his exploits. He was impressed by the way he looked and carried himself. "Sit and we'll palaver some." He took a bottle out of the drawer and two glasses and poured each about half full and shoved one toward Tye. "Have a snort first. Heard you had quit scouting and were giving the outlaws holy hell," Hruska said smiling. "Bout time someone did." He took a sip. "What brings you down here?"

El Diablo

"Ever hear of a man Named Jeb Summers?"

Hruska shook his head. "Can't say I have."

That didn't surprise Tye because he hadn't either till a few days ago. "How about El Diablo?"

Hruska almost spilled his drink which had been half way to his lips. He sat the glass back down. "Hell, everyone has heard of that infernal killer. Why do you ask?"

"Been on his trail for awhile. My partner is laid up with one of his bullets in him at Fort Clark and he dang near got me." He shoved his hat to one side so the bullet burn showed.

"That was close," Hruska said leaning some to looking at the wound. "But why are you here?"

I tracked him here. He probably came in about two hours or so ago."

"El Diablo…here?" Hruska questioned. "W..What does he look like?"

"Five foot eight or nine and one hundred fifty or so pounds. Black hair to his shoulders and dark skinned. Looks more Apache than Mexican. May be wearing the white pants and blouse that the Mexicans wear because I found a teenage Mexican boy about two miles out of town that had been killed and his clothes taken."

Hruska jumped to his feet knocking his chair over and startling Tye. "Dad-blame-it. I knew there was something about that man."

"What man? Who are you talking about? Tye stood up surprised at what a change had come over the sheriff. He was hopping mad and started for the door. "Come on Marshal. I know where that bastard is." Just as they started out of the office one of Hruska's deputies walked in.

Hruska took down a shotgun off the wall by the door and spoke to his deputy. "Joe, get ten or twelve men, men that can shoot and place a couple on every road out of this town and do it now," Joe started to turn and leave but was stopped by a hand on his shoulder and turned around. "Joe, this is Tye Watkins from Fort Clark and he has tracked the man known as El Diablo here to Eagle Pass. Tell the men that and to stop anyone leaving they don't know but be careful doing it. I don't have to tell you how dangerous this man is. And Joe, do it quietly and not obvious to everyone. I don't need a bunch of panicked people running everywhere.".

"El Diablo...here?" Joe questioned. Both men nodded and he turned and left.

"Before we go off half cocked Sheriff let's think things out and get a plan or a lot of innocent people may get hurt...or killed."

Hruska replaced the shotgun. "You're right. The man I think you are after was in the saloon twenty or so minutes ago. I questioned him for awhile like I do all strangers but he seemed okay." He slammed his fist on the desk.

"Calm down Sheriff. You had no way of knowing and if you had bucked him and not known who he was you and some others might have been killed."

"I can take care of myself Watkins," Hruska said in a stern voice.

"I know you can and I didn't mean for you to take it that way. I have heard stories about you but what I am saying is that you might have confronted what you thought was just another Mexican that knew nothing about gunplay or killing and you might have been surprised and found out to late who you were dealing with. That's what I meant."

Hruska nodded his head. "You might be right about that." He chuckled. "I caught some lead a few years ago from a man I thought was harmless. Damn near died. Should have been a lesson to me."

"Lets give Joe a few minutes to get the men set and then we'll stroll down to the saloon and have a look-see at this gent." He picked up his glass and downed the rest of the whiskey. They waited ten minutes and left the office and walked to the saloon. Both men adjusted their holsters and lifted their Colt out and dropped them back in to make sure they were not stuck in too deep so they could not be drawn quickly. Tye shut his eyes for a few seconds to let his eyes adjust from the bright sunlight. They walked through the bat wing doors of the saloon.

McMillan

El Diablo

Chapter Fifteen

Jeb recognized Tye as soon as the two lawmen entered the saloon and drew his Colt from under his shirt and fired at Tye. Tye saw the movement and stepped to one side. Tye's Colt was in his hand and firing before he even thought about it...just a reflex action. One of his slugs hit its target striking Jeb high on the left side of his chest the force of the heavy piece of lead knocking Jeb against the back wall. Hruska caught the slug intended for Tye.

Tye reached the outlaw in two quick strides and as Jeb tried to raise the Colt in his right hand Tye kicked it from his hand. Jerking the smaller man to his feet he back handed him across the mouth and set him in a chair. He turned to the men that had been sitting at some of the tables but were now standing wondering what the hell was going on.

"I'm Tye Watkins, U.S. Marshal and that man is wanted for countless murders. Maybe you have heard of him…El Diablo. I need one of yo…

He was interrupted by a young man shouting, "That Son-of-a-bitch killed by father." He had his knife out and running toward Jeb when Tye grabbed his shoulder and spun him around. The man took a swing at Tye with the knife and Tye stepped back sucking in his belly and then unleashed a right that caught the man on the point of the chin and knocked him five feet backwards and out cold.

"Like I was saying I need one of you men to hold a gun on my prisoner and make sure he doesn't do anything stupid. I want to see him hang, hopefully real slow like." Two men stepped forward with their Colts out.

"One of the men said, "Don't you fret none about him, Tye. We'll make sure he doesn't even blink." As usual a murmur had gone around the room among the men when they realized who the marshal was.

"One of you men go get a doctor," Tye said as he helped Hruska to his feet and into a chair. He ripped the shirt open and looked at the wound. It was low enough to miss the collar bone and exited out the back which was good. The hole in front was small but the exit wound was the size of a twenty dollar gold piece.

Hruska grimaced, "Did you get him"?

"He's down. Not dead but he's out of commission."

Hruska nodded. "Wasn't much help was I?" He said, sweat popping out on his forehead as the shock was wearing off and the pain was setting in. Tye patted the man on the shoulder.

"You'll be fine Sheriff. Down for awhile and sore, but you will be good as new in two or three weeks.

A voice came from across the room. "Watkins, you gonna get me a damn doctor?' Jeb's head rocked back as a young cowboy hit him in the mouth." "You'll get a damn doctor after the sheriff is taken care of and the man that Tye knocked out who was gonna carve you into little pieces for killing his father you piece of horseshit."

Tye smiled and looked at Hruska who had seen and heard what the cowboy had said and done and was attempting to smile but failing miserably. Tye patted him again on his good shoulder just as the doors swung open and the doctor came in.

In a few minutes Hruska's wound was cleaned, bandaged, and his arm in a sling. He checked the cowboy Tye had slugged and pronounced him okay and went over to Jeb to look at his wound.

Tye walked over to the young cowboy he had slugged. "You okay cowboy?"

"Feel like I got hit by a bull buffalo with a full head of steam. Damn Sir, you can hit hard. Been In lots of fights, won some and lost some, but damn I've never been hit like that," he answered rubbing his jaw.

"Glad you're okay. I didn't want to arrest you for killing my prisoner even though he deserves it."

"Sorry Marshal. I sorter lost it when you said who he was. That piece of horseshit cut my father's throat for no damn good reason."

Tye patted him on the shoulder. "Sorry for the loss of your father, but I can promise you he is going to pay for killing your father and a lot of others."

Tye walked over to where the doctor had Jeb lying on the bar working on his wound and not doing it too gently. The outlaw was complaining about the way the doc was doctoring him calling him some vile names so the young cowboy who had hit him earlier hit him again.

"I'll hit you again Jeb if you don't put a hobble on that lip of yours and shut up, but if the look Jeb gave him could kill the young cowboy would not see another sunset.

"This man is going to need be bedridden for a few days Marshal at least till he gets some strength back. He's lost a lot of blood," the doc said turning to Tye.

"Got just the place Tye, "Hruska said. "Nice roomy cell with all the comforts of home."Tye nodded and ask the barkeep to get him, the sheriff, the doctor, and the young cowboy he had slugged a drink.

El Diablo

"I don't expect you to charge anything for them either," Tye said then added when the barkeep stopped and looked at him, "I figure you will think of a way to make a lot of money off the fact this is where the famous El Diablo was captured." He laughed and added, "Hell, I figure by the time you tell the story over and over you are going to be the hero of the whole thing." Everyone laughed including a sorry attempt by the sheriff. He quickly quit and grimaced in pain.

"Tye can you help me to my office?" He turned to one of the men standing there. "Ed, can you and another man get Jeb to the jail." "Sure enough Sheriff." Tye helped Hruska and the two men carried Jeb down the block to the jail. Hruska lay down gently on his bed which was in the office and Jeb was laid on a bed in one of the cells. Tye got the keys and checked Jeb for weapons and found the knife much to Jed's consternation.

"You okay Sheriff?" Tye asked after locking the cell door on Jeb's cell.

"Yeah, just give me a glass and that bottle of rotgut in my drawer and I won't feel a thing in a little while." Tye smiled and got the bottle and glass and gave it to him knowing that the best thing for him now was to get a little whiskey in him and some sleep.

"Where can a man get something to eat?" Tye asked realizing he hadn't eaten anything since before daylight and that was a biscuit and some jerky.

I'll show you Marshal," the man named Ed said and started out the door with Tye and the young cowboy following.

The word had spread like wildfire about El Diablo being captured but most of the excitement was from the fact that Tye Watkins, the famous scout from Fort Clark was here and had captured him. People were pointing and whispering as the three men walked down the street and into a place called "Ma's Home Cooking".

"I like the name," Tye said.

Ed chuckled. "Just wait till you eat her apple pie."

The food was good that day and was also the several times Tye ate there in the next week while he waited for Jeb's wound to heal enough to travel back to Fort Clark. While in Eagle Pass Tye was treated for the most part as a celebrity. He spent a lot of time with different groups of people answering questions about his life and that of his pa and of course, Buff. He was interviewed by the paper and had a nice article written about him and the capture of El Diablo.

He and Sheriff Hruska spent a lot of time talking and Tye had even more respect for the man. Hruska was a hard man doing a hard job in a rough town, but he was as honest as the day was long and treated everyone the same no matter how important they might be. That fact, Tye believed, was the reason he kept getting re-elected by a population made up by mostly Mexicans.

El Diablo

Tye hired the young cowboy, Ed Jacobs, who had slugged Jeb, to help watch the jail and then also to ride with him to Fort Clark with the prisoner. It was only a two day trip but a extra pair of eyes would help especially when they camped for the night. Tye knew Jeb would do everything in his power to keep from having a date with the hangman. Things should be okay but he had been out here long enough to know nothing ever went exactly as planned.

McMillan

Chapter Sixteen

At Fort Clark things were not going well. Apache
trouble to the south and reported trouble to the north was
keeping Major Thurston busy dispatching patrols, taking
reports from returning patrols, writing letters to families of
soldiers killed, and taking care of the thousand and one
other problems that occur every day. He was more than
pleased with the work of the Seminole Scouts, but damn, he
missed Tye. It had been a long time since Tye had retired
as a scout and become a U.S. Marshal and a lot of scouts
had come and gone, but none so far could hold a candle to
what Tye could do. Right now he was short handed as far
as number of troops on the fort. He had two patrols to the
south, one west, and two to the north. Counting officers and
scouts that was about seventy or so men gone from the fort.

El Diablo

He was thankful for his having some good, solid officers like Captain McClellan and Lieutenant John Bullis, but most of the other officers were unproven as far as being battle tested. Seemed like he spent way too much of his time worrying and waiting on word from the patrols he had sent out and writing letter to widows or mothers.

Things were fine at the Watkins home. Little Ben and Nicole would soon be three years old, Buff has settled in being the best grandpa ever and Rebecca was happier than she had ever been. Her life would be perfect if it wasn't for the fact Tye was gone so much. She knew it was killing him not being around the children more than he was, but that was the nature of his profession. She missed him tremendously and sometimes worried herself sick, but she had known what Tye was when she married him and she loved him for it. He would always be helping others whether it was protecting them from the Apache or tracking down the men who preyed on others. She would never change him nor would she try. She would raise the kids, worry about her husband and appreciate the time they could spend together.

Lieutenant John Bullis along with three of his Seminole Scouts, Sgt. John Ward, Pvt. Pompey Factor, and trumpeter Isaac Payne lay on a knoll looking down at a Comanche camp of about thirty warriors. The soldiers had been sent to investigate the reports of Indian trouble along the Rio Grande. They had come across the tracks of a large group of unshod ponies and had tracked them to where they were now, at the junction of the Rio Pecos and Rio Grande rivers about seventy five or so miles from Fort Clark. The date was April 25th, 1875.

Being outnumbered was no deterrent to young Lt. Bullis and the scouts; seemed every time they encountered the Apache or the Comanche they were outnumbered. Bullis had the men spread out among the rocks to give an appearance of more men than their four. They opened fire on the surprised Comanche's and a fierce fire-fight took place for about forty-five minutes before the Comanche figured out they were just a few soldiers and quickly begin to surround them. Bullis saw this and ordered a retreat.

As the soldiers mounted their horses and started to make their escape they saw that their lieutenant was on the ground after his mount had bolted and ran off. Rather than make their escape they reined their mounts around and raced back to where Bullis was and as Factor and Payne laid down covering fire Ward raced in to where Bullis was and as the Comanche were closing in for the kill Bullis leapt on the back of Wards horse and all four men raced away. Bullets were splitting the air all around them and one shattered the stock of Wards rifle and another cut one of his reins. Bullis was so moved by the men's actions when they could have escaped he recommended them for medals.

El Diablo

Authors Note: Bullis's career at Fort Clark was star studded. His exploits, along with the Black Seminole Scouts he commanded were well documented and when he surrendered the command of the scouts in 1881 the grateful citizens of West Texas and of Kinney Country presented him with engraved gold and silver swords which are on display today at the Witte Museum in San Antonio.

**The three men received the Medal of Honor for saving Bullis and are buried in the Seminole Cemetery near Fort Clark along with the other Black Seminole Scouts and their families. Their graves can be seen today in the Seminole Cemetery located south west of the fort.

Several days had passed since the capture of the man known as El Diablo and Sheriff Ruska's wound had healed enough that he was up and around tending to his duties as sheriff of Eagle Pass. He and Tye had become well acquainted with each other in the past week and each held the others respect. As far as Jeb was concerned, the doc had said he could be well enough to be traveling tomorrow and that was exactly what Tye was going to do if the weather allowed him to. To the west tremendous thunderheads could be seen building up and everyone knew it was going to storm later in the day and probably be, as one old timer said, a real 'doozie'.

Later, Tye was sitting at a table in the restaurant eating a piece of Ma's delicious apple pie contemplating on what makes a man take the path hat Jeb had taken. He could understand the vengeance part of wanting to get back at whoever had done him wrong. He could relate to this because not long ago he had been the same way when his nephew was almost beaten to death, but he was looking for one man to punish not just anyone he happen to come across. Jeb had turned just plumb vicious, killing indiscriminately with no remorse or feeling for anything he did.

The door of the restaurant opened and Sheriff Hruska walked in, saw Tye and sat down at the table with the marshal.

"Looked like you were in deep thought, Marshal."

Tye smiled, "Not really I was just pondering on why a man turns bad, I mean really bad like Jeb did."

"Don't know the answer to that Tye but my pa always told me that a man can be born bad just like a man born with crooked teeth. How many times have you seen a family of several kids and all grow up to be upstanding citizens except one and no one know why that one turned out to be a sour apple, always in trouble." He sat back in his chair as a cup of coffee was set before him by a young lady that Tye figured to be Ma's granddaughter. "Maybe the good Lord makes men like that every once in awhile so men like me and you who can't do anything else will have a job," he chuckled.

Tye laughed. "Hadn't ever thought of it that way." He laughed again and added, "Maybe you're right about that."

"I did hear a story about Jeb awhile back, but don't know if would hold water or not," Hruska said. "The way I heard it was that some Mexicans raided his camp while he was away and killed his mother, children, and raped and killed his wife. He had not been a problem to anyone before that and he lived with the Apache for a few years before the killing of his wife and child gaining a reputation as a warrior of high status. It was after the killing then that he started his rampage."

"That's pretty much the way I heard it. After his family was killed he lived with an aunt for three or four years then she was killed by soldiers who raided their peaceful village. That snapped something inside him and here he is now, set to hang for no telling how many murders. I believe he sh..."Tye was interrupted by a tremendous clap of thunder that shook the walls of the restaurant.

Both men hit the door and rushed outside to see where the lightning had struck because it had to have been close. They were driven back inside by the wind and rain which was coming down in sheets and with the wind was coming almost horizontal.

"Damn Hruska," Tye hollered above the wind and rain. "This is the worst storm I ever saw in my whole dad blame life." He started to say more but was drowned out by a roar that sounded like a freight train.

"What the…" Hruska shouted but was cut off by Tye's shoving him back thru the door and onto the floor and shouting.. "Stay down."

"Twister!" someone shouted. The two men hugged the floor along with some others in the restaurant as the noise increased and the building began to shake. Glass from the shattered windows flew through the room like knives cutting and sticking in everything, furniture, walls, and a couple of men. A minute later the only sound was the sound of rain on the roof of the one story restaurant. Tye and the others stood up and made their way to the door dreading what they would find outside.

The scene was worse than the men expected. The buildings on the opposite side of the street were flatten, some completely gone except for the floors. Several horses were dead and others injured so bad men were shooting them which to a cowboy is almost like killing ones family member.

Tye stepped into the middle of the street and looked south toward where the stable was he had Sandy in and was relieved to see it standing. Hruska uttered a loud curse.

"Damn! The jail is bout gone." Both men ran up the street to where the jail stood or what was left of it. The front wall and part of the roof was almost completely gone. Inside the office was a mess, desk and chairs overturned, papers lying on the floor or plastered to the walls. The door leading to the cells was off its hinges and both men rushed in to check on the breed. The first thing they saw was Joe, Hruska's deputy, lying on the floor in a pool of blood. The cell door was open and it was empty. El Diablo was gone.

"What happened Joe," Hruska asked the deputy as he kneeled and turned the deputy onto his back and was surprised the man was still alive. A hole in his chest showed he had been shot.

Joe's eyes fluttered then opened. His hand grasped Hruska's arm. "Sa...Saw the twister co...coming and kn...knew it was gon...knew it was gonna hit the jail" He closed his eyes for a second and gasped, a wheezing sound coming from his throat and foamy blood came from the corner of his mouth. "I...I opened the cell door to take Je... to take Jeb out of the building. The son-of-a-bitch jerked my pistol out and shot m...me." He was struggling to breathe now and both men knew it was only a matter of seconds before the man would be gone.

Joe suddenly seemed to gain strength and looked at Tye and spoke almost in a whisper. "Sorry Tye. Sh...Should have just le...left the man in the cel..." he didn't finish as he gasped one more time and died.

Hruska stood up. "Joe's been my deputy for three years and no sheriff ever had a better one." He tried to hold back his grief but could not. " he...he was my best friend too," he mumbled. Tye placed his hand on the man's trembling shoulder and walked back to the office to let Hruska get the grief out of his system in private.

The first thing he noticed was the open drawer in the over turned desk. It was the drawer where Jeb's gun, holster, and knife had been. He rushed outside and looked up and down the street but saw only stunned and dazed town folk. He ran down the street to the stables only to find the livery man lying on the floor in a pool of blood. Tye kneeled and turned him over and the man's head lay at a weird angle. His throat had been cut so deep he had almost been decapitated.

Sheriff Hruska walked into the livery stable at that moment and saw the livery man lying on the floor his head almost cut off.

"What the hell?"

Tye stood up and looked at the sheriff. "Jeb sheriff. That's his trademark," Tye said pointing to the almost severed head.

"My God," Hruska mumbled.

"Since the livery man is dead I need to know if any horses are missing," Tye asked as he checked on Sandy. He saddled Sandy as Hruska looked at the horses in the other stalls.

Hruska walked around the man on the floor and looked in the corral and then each stall.

"Damn that bastard," he shouted. "He took the best damn horse in the whole town.

El Diablo

Tye looked at the highly upset man. "Mine. The son-of-a-bitch took my horse."

"I'll get him back and bring him to you," Tye said knowing how the man felt. A man's horse out here was usually not just thought of as a means of getting around, but a horse was a companion and friend on the lonely nights on the trail. They were loyal to their master and a lot of times would save their master's tail by getting him away from danger or maybe just warn him through his actions of danger. Some men like Tye, actually talked to their horses or sang some of the ballads that were popular at the time. A popular saying was "I guess my singing is okay cause my horse never complains."

"You won't have to bring him to me Marshal because I'm going with you."

"I know how you feel Hruska, but your place is here. A lot of these people lost everything, even family members today. Don't you think they are going to need you, need someone to show them what they need to do, someone strong and thinking straight. Besides all that there will be a few that will try and take advantage of the situation and take things that don't belong to them from the stores that are damaged." He stepped into the saddle and settled his butt in the seat of the saddle. "What did your horse look like?"

"Big-as big as your horse," Hruska said stepping back and looking at Sandy. "He's black as the ace of spades. The only spot that's not black is his mane. For some reason he has streaks of silver mixed in with the black."

"Anything about his tracks I need to know so I can pick them out from others?"

Hruska thought for a moment. "Not really," he paused then snapped his fingers as a thought came to him. "Left rear shoe was loose. That's the reason he was in a stall and not the corral. "Old Joe there," he said nodding to the man on the floor, "was going to shoe it, but whether he did or not I don't know."

"I'm betting he didn't or your horse would have been in the corral." Tye stooped some and laid Sandy's neck on his shoulder and scratched him with both hands. "Bet you were a little nervous a few minutes ago wasn't' you boy?" Sandy nickered. Tye smiled. Leading Sandy over to where Hruska stood he said. "You can help me one more time Sheriff by walking down the west edge of town and see if there are any tracks in the wet ground. I don't figure Jeb left town by the road so I'll take the east edge of town and look for tracks. Fire one shot if you find anything."

Hruska nodded and the two men went their separate ways. Five minutes later Tye heard the familiar blast of a Colt and reined Sandy that way making his way around the fallen buildings, fences and dazed people that were digging through the rubble looking for something or someone. I'd love to help these people but if I don't corral Jeb quick more people will die by his hand.

El Diablo

He found Hruska and dismounted looking at the tracks. Tye smiled as he looked at the track of the left rear hoof. Jeb wasn't going far because the shoe had not been fixed, in fact from the looks of the tracks it was almost coming off.

"Looks like he will be afoot fore long," Hruska said.

"Sorter looks that way." He reached down and extended his hand which Hruska took. "Been nice meeting you Sheriff. It's always good meeting an honest lawmen. There's a lot that are not. You know."

Hruska nodded. "Met a few of them. You take care Tye and and bring that murdering bastard back." He released Tye's hand. "Guess I'd better get the townsfolk together and get a plan in place to help each other clean up this mess." Tye straightened up in the saddle, tipped his hat and rode off following Jeb's tracks.

Hruska watched him ride off. *There's a man if I ever saw one. I do believe ever damn story I ever heard about him is probably true,* he thought. "Watch over him Lord cause we need men like that out here," he said out loud looking up at the heavy clouds that promised more rain.

Chapter Seventeen

Jeb was cussing his bad luck with gusto. His mount was limping badly and he found the shoe that was almost off.

"Of all the horses in the livery I had to pick you," he said in a very frustrated voice as he stripped the saddle and blanket from his back and threw them behind some brush. He slapped the horse on the rump with the barrel of his Henry and the horse took off like a scalded dog even with the bad hoof.

He studied the terrain around him with the eyes of man that was desperate to find a quick route to the river and Mexico. After a minute and with no luck he just took off west in that easy lope that only an Apache possessed that could cover miles without stopping. He figured Watkins, if he survived the storm would be after me quickly. *I figure he will think I will take the shorter route to the river so I will angle to the south a little. May be a little farther than it is now but he will catch me with that horse of his if I don't try and fool him some.* While moving through the mesquite, cactus and sage careful to leave as few signs as possible he thought about what happened in Eagle Pass. *That twister was a stroke of luck as was that stupid deputy who tried to help me. If my luck was really good maybe the storm killed that damned Watkins. No, he thought again, that would be too much of a good thing to expect. I'm gonna have to act as if he is on my trail right now and with the wet ground even my moccasins are leaving tracks a blind man could follow. I'll find a place to fort up and if Watkins is on my trail I should know quickly and maybe I can take care of him with the Henry and then mosey on over to Mexico and take my chances with the stupid Federales.*

Tye kneeled on the ground studying the tracks of the horse and of Jeb. "Looks like Hruska's horse went lame and Jeb's on foot now, Sandy," he said standing up and forking the saddle. Knowing Jeb was half Apache he knew that being without a horse wasn't much of a problem. An Apache could out distance a horse over the long haul but the good thing was the tracks were no more than an hour old so Sandy might just be able to catch him since the tracks are as plain as day and he could follow them even at a gallop.

Thirty minutes had passed when Jeb saw who he figured was Watkins following his tracks. He was still a mile away so he had time to get in a shooting position that was comfortable. When he looked again after getting in position he was surprised Tye was no more than a hundred fifty yards away and coming at a fast gallop.

He centered the 'v' of his rifle barrel on the man's chest and exhaled while slowly putting pressure on the trigger. The Henry bucked against his shoulder and the bullet sped toward its target no more than a hundred yards away. *No way can I miss at this range*, Jeb thought as he pulled the trigger.

An instant before Tye heard the crack of the rifle he reined Sandy to the left following the tracks which had left the due west course Jeb had been headed. The slight changing of direction saved his life as the heard bullet split the air an instant before he heard the sound of the rifle firing. He left the saddle on the opposite side of Sandy grabbing his Henry as he did and hit the ground running. Two more bullets came his way one which hit the wet ground almost under his feet and the other split a mesquite branch as he ran by it.

Glancing up the hill he got a fix where the shooter was by the smoke from the Henry that hung in the still air. He dropped to the ground and snuggled up to the base of a large cedar to catch his breath and study the area some and plan how he was going to get to the place where Jeb was holed up.

He could see no easy way after searching the area. He settled back and when his breathing was normal again he looked again. The place was sixty or seventy yards up a fairly steep slope. He could circle around and come on him from the back but he could not see how he could do it without exposing himself before he had a chance to shoot. The only way he could figure to get to him would be a frontal assault and do like the Apaches do with two quick steps and then hit the ground and wait awhile and do it again. Dangerous yes, but he could see no other way.

He studied the area between him and where Jeb was. There might just be sufficient cover. There were a few large boulders and several short cedars growing on the slope. He thought about things for a moment. *This could take awhile so I had better get me some water to carry with me.* He crawled slowly a few feet to where thick cedars were clustered together and then ran at a crouch a few feet before dropping to the ground again. He scooted on his belly to where Sandy stood chomping on some grass. Tye crawled under his horses belly and stood up just enough on the side away from Jeb to slip the canteen from the pommel. He took a swallow and jammed the cork back in and slung the rawhide strap around his neck and lay back down, the canteen resting on his back as he crawled again back to where he had been, but suddenly stopped as a thought came to him. *Jeb figures I am over there and would have his rifle trained on that spot to fire instantly at any movement. If I start up the hill from here it would take him a second or so to realize I wasn't where he thought I was and another second to aim his rifle. That might just give me time to get up the hill a ways before he can fire accurately.*

He studied the terrain for a few minutes to plan his route up the slope. His route planned out as best he could he gathered his feet under him and taking a deep breath lurched himself from behind the cedar and raced up the hill to where he had planned his first stop would be. A bullet struck a rock close to his head splattering rock fragments in his face as he dove behind another large boulder.

"Jeb is a lot quicker than I figured," he mumbled out loud. "That was close," he added wiping a little blood from his right cheek from the rock fragments.

Jeb figured this was it for him. He was trapped on the side of a hill with nowhere to go and the best, most tenacious scout in Texas coming up after him. He slipped back deeper in the stand of cedars and stripped off his white man's clothes and pulled his breechcloth, red kerchief to wrap around his head and the knee high Apache moccasins from his saddlebags which he had carried up the slope along with his canteen. He already had his knife out. *At least I can die Apache and not in the stinking white man's clothes,* he thought to himself as he dressed quickly and hurried back to where he had been hidden when he fired at Watkins. He scanned the area below him and knew he had made a mistake in the minute or so he had taken to change clothes. He now wasn't sure where the man was. He looked up at the ridge above him and was surprised he had not seen it earlier.

An opening of a cave was about forty or so feet above him. He looked back down the slope, studying every rock and bush for a sign of Watkins. Seeing none he jumped to his feet and headed up to where he had seen the opening and arriving there just as two bullets fired almost as one hit the rocks as he dove inside. He lay there catching his breath before sitting up. He looked around and knew he had made a mistake. The back of the cave was only four or so feet deep. His thoughts went to an event he had heard about that occurred a couple years earlier in Arizona where a group of Yavapai Indians were trapped in a cave and massacred by the soldiers led by General Crook who used ricochets from their bullets off the cave walls to kill most of the Yavapai. It was to be known as the Skeleton Cave Massacre. *I hope that stinking scout doesn't think about using the same trick*, he thought to himself. The thought gave him an uncomfortable feeling. That thought become a reality a minute later.

Watkins voice from below broke his train of thought. "Jeb, you might as well give up. You have no place to go. Look around you Jeb; look at the close in walls. If that cave isn't very deep I can use ricochet bullets to kill you. You ever see a wound from a bullet that has flatten out from ricocheting off rocks before striking the body. It's an ugly sight and dang painful I might add. Use your head and come out with your hands up and I'll see to it that you get a fair trial."

The words 'fair trial' brought a laugh from Jeb's lips. He yelled back. "Hanging is no way for an Apache to die. Fighting his enemies is the only good death for an Apache warrior." He rose up firing his Henry as fast as he could pull the trigger and lever in a new shell keeping Tye's head down. He moved toward the crest of the hill behind him as he fired and was moving over the top when his gun clicked on an empty chamber. He began shoving in new ones as he moved down the slope.

Tye knew what Jeb was doing but had no choice but to keep his head down as bullets careened off the boulder he was behind as well as scattering a thousand rock fragments. He felt something wet on his back and knew one of the ricochets had punctured his canteen. When the firing slowed he took a quick look over the boulder and caught a glimpse of Jeb's head going down the other side of the hill. Cursing he checked his rifle to make sure he had shells and rushed toward the crest of the hill.

Reaching the top he crawled to take a look on the other side keeping his head below the sage and cactus. He saw Jeb about a hundred yards below him and moving fast away from him. He fired three quick shots at the fleeing outlaw but knew with shooting downhill and Jeb moving side to side dodging boulders and cactus there was a small chance of hitting him. He was right.

He stood and took off running down the slope keeping his eyes both on the ground and on Jeb to make sure the killer didn't stop, turn and fire at him. His long strides were making up ground and when he hit the bottom of the hill he was only sixty or so yards behind Jeb. He saw Jeb look over his shoulder at him and then the man took off at a run instead of a fast trot. Tye knew this wasn't going to be easy or quick as Jeb was now an Apache and nothing on earth was as dangerous as a cornered Apache. He could have shot the man in the back a minute ago, but that wasn't

El Diablo

Tye. Shooting a man in the back was a last resort as far as he was concerned.

As he ran Tye took stock of the situation. He had ammunition but no food and no water. The food was no big deal but the water was. He knew Jeb was in the same fix and no water out here could kill you as sure as a bullet, just not as quick. *This needs to end pretty quick before I get too far from Sandy and the extra canteen*, he thought to himself. He picked up the pace dodging cactus, sage and mesquite while keeping his eyes on the running Jeb.

As he angled left to go around a large mesquite only quick reflexes born from all his years surviving out here saved him. A large rattlesnake was coiled, head back and ready to strike lay in his path where his next step would be. Without thinking he leapt in the air and came down maybe a foot behind the snake and kept moving even though he was a little more than shaken over the close call.

Of a sudden Jeb stopped, turned and fired his Henry. Reflexes that saved him from the rattler worked again for Tye. As Jeb's rifle came up he dove to the left as the bullet split the air harmlessly over head. He brought his rifle up and fired twice, but hit nothing but air as Jeb had hit the ground as soon as he fired at Tye. Tye reached to his belt and took out some shells and fed them into the Henry. He slid his Colt out and checked the loads in it and made sure it was in working order. He glanced at his right boot to make sure his Bowie was still there. He thought to himself that I may need them all before this is over. He glanced up at the sun. Probably about five o'clock. *This situation could get real nasty after dark with that sneaky piece of horse dung out there. Somehow, someway I have to end this before then, he mused.*

The situation was desperate for both men. One wanted nothing more than to kill the other and one wanted to capture the other or kill him only if necessary. They were fifty or sixty yards apart with nothing but short sage bushes, cactus, three and four foot cedars and a occasional mesquite between them.

Tye had his buckskin shirt on which blended in with the surroundings and Jeb's brown skin blended in also. This was going to come down to whom could injun up on the other. Tye lay on his side watching the brush in front of him. He took off his hat and placed it on a stick and lifted it just above the tops of the sage and cactus and moved it like he was crawling. A bullet smashed the hat just below the head band. Tye saw the smoke.

"There you are," he mumbled and leaving his hat started crawling slowly to his left wanting to get behind the outlaw. He had left his Henry with his hat and had the Colt in his hand as he figured if there was shooting it would be close in. Besides, the rifle would hinder him in crawling and scooting along the ground.

He was sweating profusely and that worried him as sweat was moisture leaving his body and he needed all of that he could keep within with no water to drink. He was moving very slow, careful to make no noise or raise any dust that could be seen or heard. His mouth was dry so he picked up a small pebble and placed it in his mouth which caused his saliva glands to produce a little moisture which helped, but he knew it was short term answer to the dry mouth and parched throat.

He kept moving steadily always careful not to scrape any rocks loose and keeping his head below the tops of the sage. For one hour he crawled and scooted on the hot ground only occasionally stopping to get his bearings. There was no sound other than the soft whisper of the mesquite leaves stirring in the light breeze that had come up suddenly. Finally he figured he had gone far enough and moved to his right toward where he figured Jeb lay. Two minutes later he cursed under his breath.

"Damn him to hell." He saw where the outlaw had been finding the shell casing from Jeb's Henry. He's trying to get behind me too and just went the opposite direction I did. Raising his head to take a look he saw Jeb looking at him from where he had been earlier. He dropped his head just as a bullet buzzed by where he head had been followed by two more that kicked up dust and rocks just in front of him. He rolled to his right and came up firing his pistol at Jeb who was moving up the slope at a fast pace and dodging obstacles which did not give Tye much of a shot. It was then he realized what Jeb had in mind.

"The son-of-a-bitch is going to try and get to Sandy and the water," he cursed then laughed under his breath. "He's going to be in for a shock when he tries to mount Sandy." He stood and started running his long legs again eating up the distance between him and his quarry. When he topped the hill he stepped quickly to his right and this saved his life again.

Jeb fired just as Tye topped the hill. Tye stepped to his right at the same instant and the bullet cut a quarter inch deep gash across his left shoulder. He fired his Colt and saw the dust fly from Jeb's left pants leg then watched as the man lost his balance and fell down and then tumbled a few feet down the slope. He came to his feet, fired another shot at Tye and then turned and rushed down the slope paying little attention to his leg wound.

Tye was rushing down the hill not paying attention to obstacles but keeping his eyes on Jeb expecting him to turn and fire at him again. He was forty or so yards from the bottom of the slope when Jeb reached Sandy. The outlaw triggered two rounds at Tye but fired too quickly and missed. He jerked Sandy's reins free and leaped in the saddle. A second later he was in mid air after Sandy bucked hard getting all four hooves off the ground. Jeb hit hard on his back stunning him and would have left most men lying there gasping for air, but not Jeb. He was a hard man, a tough man, and had not survived all the chases he had been in with the law and Federales by being otherwise. His problem now was his leg wound and not regaining all his strength back from the chest wound almost three weeks ago.

Hurting as he was he came to his feet and was face to face with Tye who was crouched fifteen feet away with his Colt in his hand. Jeb raised his Henry to fire even though he felt Tye had him dead to rights. Both men pulled the triggers at the same time with the same results, hammers falling on empty chambers. Tye holstered his Colt and drew his Bowie from the sheath in top of his right boot. Jeb dropped the Henry and pulled his knife from the sheath on his belt.

Tye noticed the bloody hole in Jeb's leg just above the left knee where his bullet had gone through. It was bleeding but not severe enough to hamper Jeb's fighting ability which Tye figured was going to be good. His own left arm hurt like hell mostly from sweat running into the deep crease. Both men dropped into a crouch and circled each other from left to right.

"So you are the great scout that has my people so afraid," he said his voice low, and menacing. "The great scout that cannot be killed but I see you bleed like any man," his eyes glancing at the wound on Tye's upper arm. "I am going to kill you Watkins, cut off your stinking head and leave it at the bridge over Los Moras at Fort Clark. My family is dead, but I understand you have one. Maybe I take them for my family."

Tye held his temper and answered. "You gonna talk me to death Jeb or you going to try to kill me with that knife."

They had gone in a complete circle and of a sudden Jeb dropped and scooped up a handful of dirt and threw it at Tye's face. Tye shut his eyes for just a second as the dirt hit him in the face and he swept his blade blindly in a sweeping motion in front of him. Jeb barely evaded the slashing blade by stepping back instead of lunging in as he had planned.

"That's an old trick Jeb used by men who aren't good enough with the blade to fight fair." He grinned. "Now come on and fight like a man."

Enraged, Jeb lunged quickly almost catching Tye off balance, but the years of fighting Apaches with knives showed and he smiled as he easily parried Jeb's thrust and then a second thrust and then hit the outlaw with a smashing left fist in the mouth. Jeb staggered back and then fell hard on his back. He was barely conscious of the man standing over him. He blinked several times and shook his head to clear the cobwebs. His eyes finally focused on Tye who was squatting near him and the marshal said chuckling.

"For a supposedly bad man you sure do lack a lot of fighting ability. I guess I now know why you killed from ambush and from behind."

Jeb glared at the marshal started to say something very unkind but bit his tongue and asked. "How come I'm not in shackles?" knowing he had been out for a moment or so and he was curious.

"You remind me of another man I had to bring in who fancied himself to be the baddest man around. Man by the name of Yancey Cates. He was a cold blooded killer just like you. You are like him in that neither of you have any regards for a human life and both were mostly all mouth. I felt he wanted to prove just how tough he was. He caused a lot of pain and suffering not only to those he killed but to the families just like you have and I figured he needed to suffer some just like you do and I intend to see to it that you do."

"And?"

"He wasn't much and was a lot less when I whipped him for the third time. Finally got to see him hang just like you probably will."

Tye stood up. "Get up you piece of horse shit. Get up and let's see how much of a man you are."

Jeb slowly got to his feet. He had a feeling he was in for a bad time but be damned if he was going to go down easy. He saw his knife stuck in the ground a few feet away. Tye saw him looking at it.

"Go ahead and try to get it but if you do you'll sure as hell eat it."

Jeb knew he meant it and he probably would be eating it. It's a long ways back to Clark and a lot can happen between here and there so it's best to stay alive, he thought as he prepared to take his beating which he knew was coming. For the first time in years he was really afraid.

Tye stood in front of Jeb like a giant oak. "Take your best shot," Jeb.

Jeb unleashed a right toward Tye's chin. Tye blocked Jeb's fist with his left forearm and drove his right into Jeb's belly. Jeb's eyes bulged and one could hear the whoosh as all the air left Jeb. He doubled over gasping, frantically trying to get his breath back. He couldn't seem to get any air and he was sure he was going to die.

Tye grabbed him by the collar jerking him erect and slammed his fist into Jeb's face never letting go of the collar holding him up as Jeb's knees buckled.

"Come on tough guy," he growled his face only inches from Jeb's. Jeb was still trying to get some air and was as limp as a rag doll. "If you ain't about the sorriest excuse for an Apache I ever did see." He loosened his grip on the man's collar and Jeb dropped to the ground and rolled up in a fetal position.

Tye walked over to Sandy and tightened the girth on his saddle which had slipped when he bucked Jeb off. He glanced over at Jeb who still lay on the ground groaning and cursing Tye, the law, and everything else with every breath. Tye took a pair of handcuffs from his saddle bag and scratched Sandy between the ears.

"Well Sandy, it looks like it might be a long ride back to Eagle Pass except for some us it will be a long walk." He laughed and scratched Sandy under the chin then walked over to Jeb with the strips to tie his hands together.

"Stand up Jeb," Tye said.

"You go straight to hell lawman," Jeb said and reached with his right hand behind his neck and came out with a straight razor slashing at Tye's throat. Tye caught off guard jerked his head back and his left hand up in an instinctive defensive move.

"Damn," Tye hollered as the blade slashed deep into his left forearm and swung his right fist without thinking catching Jeb below the left eye and opening a nasty gash. Tye grabbed his Bowie just as Jeb leaped for him slashing in a downward arc toward Tye's neck. Tye grabbed Jeb's wrist with his bloody left hand and drove his Bowie into Jeb's belly.

Jeb's eyes bulged and he stood still for a moment as Tye held his wrist with the razor in it and held the knife in the outlaw's belly. Jeb tried to say something but all that came out was gobs of blood. His eyes glazed over and Tye released his wrist and jerked his Bowie out of Jeb's belly letting the man fall to the ground.

He looked at his forearm and cursed. "Going to be damn sore, Sandy. Damn sore." He took a clean shirt and using his Bowie cut some strips and wrapped them tightly around his forearm to stop the flow of blood. It slowed some but not enough and he knew he could be in trouble if it didn't.

He collected Jeb's pistol and knives and put them in his saddle bag. He slid the Henry into the leather and mounted Sandy. He looked down at Jeb. "I'll send someone for you Jeb. Even a low life like you doesn't deserve to be food for the critters out here.

McMillan

Thirty minutes later his arm was still bleeding a lot so he reined in Sandy and took a strip of rawhide and wrapped it around his upper arm and using his right hand tied a knot. He twisted the knot it to make it tighter and as he did watched as the blood flow seem to slow. He was glad because he was becoming a little light headed.

Tye was still five or so miles from Eagle Pass, it was hot and he drank the last of his water as they headed for town. An hour later he could see the town on the horizon, but for some reason he could not focus his eyes very well. The blood had slowed but never stopped and he felt himself losing consciousness. He leaned down and spoke in Sandy's ear. "It's up to you big boy...get us to town." He tried to smile when Sandy nickered but failed. He nudged Sandy forward, leaned forward in the saddle, his head resting on Sandy's neck, passed out.

El Diablo

Chapter Eighteen

Tye opened his eyes, looked around and trying to figure out where he was. He was in a bed, his arm bandaged and in a sling. He heard voices in the next room.

"From what the Indian said it must have been a hell of a fight from the sign he read."

Tye recognized the voice as that of Sheriff Hruska. "Hruska. Get your tail in here."

Hruska walked into the room with another man who was much older, probably in his sixties.

Hruska said. "Welcome back to the land of the living Marshal. You had us worried for awhile."

Tye shook the man's hand and Hruska said. "Tye, this here is Bill Clements. Bill's a doctor and he's the one who patched you up."

Tye shook the man's hand. "Thanks Doc. I owe you." He looked at Sheriff Hruska. "You need to send a man to get the body of Jeb."

"Already done Tye. Sent a friend of mine who is Apache. He back tracked your horse to the body."

Tye was confused. "When…how long have I been out?"

"He brought the body in late yesterday. You've been out since day before yesterday."

"Where is the body?"

"Buried in our grave yard for outlaws and other no accounts. I made note of the body, its wounds etc. Looks like he ran into a tree a few times."

Tye smiled. "He caused a lot of pain and misery for a lot of people. I figured he needed a little misery too."

"You sure enough did that."

"He should have lived to hang but when I went to tie his hands he came up with a razor from a sheath behind his neck."

"That where the cut came?"

"Yeah. He damn near got my throat and would have if not for a reflex action with my arm coming up without me even thinking. Thinks went downhill for him after that."

"The main thing is that the son-of-a-bitch is dead and you're alive."

Tye looked at the two men. "I won't forget this and both of you will be mentioned in my report."

Tye remembered the storm. "How many were killed in the storm?"

The doctor spoke up. "We were lucky Tye. Seventeen were killed and about one hundred hurt most not seriously which was bad but nothing near what it could have been. He put his hand on Hruska's shoulder. "Sheriff Hruska took command of the search for the dead and injured and then held a meeting on how we would recover and rebuild. I figure he has a job here for as long as he wants."

Tye smiled and said. "I know he has. I wish I would run into more sheriffs like him." He looked back at the doctor. "How long before I can travel. I have a wife and two kids I need to see."

"I figure maybe two days three at the most."

Tye laid his head back on the pillow and thoughts of Rebecca, Nicole, and little Ben were racing around in his mind.

He thought of this marshaling job and how it kept him away from his family so much, a lot more than he had expected. He was gone a lot scouting for the army, but it was usually only one to four days at a time not three or so weeks like he had been on Jeb's trail. He definitely had some thinking to do and he and Rebecca needed to have another long talk about his and their future.

Three days later Tye sat on Sandy and reaching down shook Sheriff Hruska's hand.

"It's been a pleasure meeting you Sheriff," he said. He looked around at the town that was already petty much cleaned up after the storm and with new buildings going up. "You did a great job in holding these people together after the twister and getting them to start over. "

"Thanks Tye," Hruska replied. "These are good people and I think this town is gonna be bigger and better than ever and I want to be part of it."

"Well, with what the doc said the other day I figure you have a job here as long as you want it," Tye said. "I wish all the towns had sheriffs as honest and dedicated as you are."

"We'll see what the future holds. If I learned anything over the years wearing this badge it's that some people have short memories and what's said today don't hold water tomorrow," Hruska answered chuckling.

Tye smiled knowing what the man said was true. "Well if they forget what you done here you just contact me and I'll come running to remind them." He reined

El Diablo

Sandy around and pointed him north toward Fort Clark. "I'll see you again Sheriff and tell the doc thanks for patching me up." He nudged Sandy and the big horse headed out of town.

Hruska watched him go just as doc walked up. "Doc there goes a man that anyone would be proud to ride the river with. With men like him chasing the bad guys just maybe this country will settle down and become a safer place for men and women to raise their families."

Epilogue

Two weeks had passed since the killing of El Diablo. Tye and Sam had both recovered from their wounds. Tye had enjoyed being fretted over by Rebecca and probably had extended his care a few days longer than necessary. He and Rebecca had discussed his marshaling job and his being gone so long at a time. He had to admit when he did come back it was a lot of fun making up for lost time as man and wife. They both decided that it was best for Tye to continue for a time until his reputation grew and he might just get a job as sheriff or town marshal in a quiet little town somewhere where the kids could go to a larger school and be around more kids their age.

Sam had come by and was wondering about the kids he had left at the Whitlock's, Billy and Elizabeth. They decided they would ride to the Whitlock's and pick up the two children and try to find a home here for them. They left early the next morning.

El Diablo

As they rode into the yard at the Whitlock's, Elizabeth spotted them and ran toward them hollering, "Billy…Billy it's Sam….Sam's back Billy."

Sam dismounted and rushed toward the little girl and swept her into his arms just as Billy came running up to them. Sam reached out and took him into his arms also and the three hugged each other. Tye stepped down from Sandy and watched.

Willie Whitlock came about that time and Sam stood up and introduced him to Tye.

"Heard a lot about you that past three or four years, Tye," Willie said reaching up and shaking the marshal's hand. Tye noticed the man had a firm grip and his hands were rough and calloused showing years of hard work. He also looked Tye in the eye when he spoke which Tye had learned over the years spoke well of a man. His pa told him never to trust a man who would not look you in the eye when speaking to you.

"Step down Tye and you two come on in the house. Elizabeth will fetch you some donuts she made herself and we'll eat, drink some coffee and palaver some.

Sitting at the table Tye could not help but notice how neat and clean the house was.

"Very nice place you have here Mrs. Whitlock."

"Thank you very much, but if you don't mind call me Millie. Mrs. Whitlock makes me feel old," she chuckled.

Tye laughed. These were typical people coming out here to make a go of it. Honest and hard working and wanting nothing more than to be left alone to live their lives.

"These are delicious Elizabeth," Sam said taking another bite of the donuts she made. Elizabeth's face had a smile as big as the Rio Grande River.

"What are you going to do with the children," Millie asked?

"Going to see if we can find them a home back at Fort Clark" Sam replied.

Millie looked at her husband who nodded his head. "The last three weeks have been the happiest of Willie's and my life. We cannot have children and these two have brought a joy to us that we haven't known before. If the children think they would be happy here we would love to raise them and love them as our own."

Sam stopped chewing and looked at Tye who had a smile on his face that would have put Elizabeth's to shame. Sam swallowed the donut and washed it down with coffee. That's great Millie…just great." He stood up and said.

"Let me talk to the kids." He walked outside followed by Billy and Elizabeth.

El Diablo

"What do you two think?"

The kids looked at each other and then back at Sam. "They are great," Billy said.

"They are really good to us Sam,"Elizabeth said reaching and holding Billy's hand.

"Do you two think you could live here and be happy?"

"Oh yes, Sam. Yes, Yes," Elizabeth cried.

"What about you Billy?"

"I'll miss my ma and pa, but the Whitlock's have taken us in like their own. Yes, we would be happy here."

"Then it's settled," Sam said then added. "A lot of times a person's real parents are stuck with children they did not want. It's a lot of responsibility raising kids. You have people like the Whitlock's and you are talking about people who want you, want the responsibility of raising you and teaching you how to do things and what is right and what is wrong. You need to remember that things get out of kilter once in a while. Life is not easy out here and things won't go always smooth so just remember they love you as their own and they picked you which make both of you special just like they are." He opened his arms and both kids came to him and they all hugged each other. Try as he might Sam could not keep the tears of happiness from rolling down his cheeks.

McMillan

Sam and Tye rode away from the Whitlock's and looked back and waved to the family knowing that the good Lord had led Sam to this home three weeks ago.

"Wonder what our next assignment will be?" Sam mumbled.

"No telling Sam," Tye answered then added. "You know that girl you're sweet on is about twenty miles west of here. If you think you wouldn't get lost you might just ride over for a surprise visit, Tye said chuckling. "I'm sure she could help you with your wound and give you some sympathy along with it."

"You think this pilgrim can't find his way. You think you're the only man around this part of the country can find his way around." Sam replied. "You know I think I will just do that," he said laughing. "See you in a couple days, Tye," he said over his shoulder as he reined his horse west.

Tye watched him ride away and reached down and scratched Sandy's neck. "You know Sandy it wouldn't surprise me one bit if old Sam there is gonna get himself hitched pretty quick." He sat up in the saddle and nudged Sandy with his heels into a gallop. "Let's go home."

El Diablo

About the Author

Gary was born in Levelland, Texas which is thirty miles due west of Lubbock just after the start of World War II. His father was in the Air Force and Gary was almost three years old before his father met his son. He was the oldest of three children having two younger sisters. He was raised by parents who were God-Fearing and the family was in Church every time the door was open. His father was a Deacon in Fifth Street Baptist Church.

In the house were two types of books and magazines; the Bible and Frontier Time magazines as well as additions of Old West and True West. These magazines laid the foundation of Gary's love of the Old West and its colorful characters and countless hours were spent reading them.

Gary played football and baseball at LHS and was lucky enough to get a football scholarship at Texas Tech University. He promptly had two knee operations which ended his athletic career.

He wrote his first book, Border Trouble, in 2002. In all of his books he has tried to show just what our great, great, grandparents went through to settle this great country we now call Texas. He hopes his readers can see this and have a greater appreciation for what those brave people did a hundred and fifty or so years ago that gave us the opportunities and the good things in life we now enjoy.

McMillan

He loves writing the Tye Watkins series and sees no end to the series as of now. He has started book number twelve which a short introduction is on the flowing pages.

El Diablo

Tye Watkins in

RANGE WAR

Book XII of the series

McMillan

Chapter One

Five weeks had passed since Tye came home after the demise of the outlaw known as El Diablo. He had been given extra leave to recover from his wounds. Five weeks of being with his wife and two kids. Every time he came home from an assignment it seemed like the kids had grown in height and weight. It had been a happy five weeks and he and Rebecca had long discussions about his future. They both decided that it might be best for him to stay a marshal a little longer and then he could find himself a nice quiet town that needed a sheriff and they would move there. It would be better for the kids as they might have a larger school to attend and many more children to be around.

Tye had a chance to visit his old friends at Clark; friends like Major Thurston, Sergeants O'Malley, Carter, and of course Sergeant Absher, and a new friend,

Lieutenant Bullis. Tye was pleased to learn that the Apache problem had quieted down some with only occasional small raiding parties coming across the Border. He learned that Bullis and his Seminole Scouts were instrumental in this fact. Now, the main concern was the Comanche who were raiding closer and closer to the fort. This was not new news of the Comanche coming south from the plains and panhandle of Texas. The fort, built around Los Moras Springs, was on the Old Comanche War Trail that had been used for generations when the Comanche headed south to raid and plunder in Mexico. The springs with its cold, clear waters and the many pecan trees was a favorite stopping place.

Tye, Rebecca, Buff, and the kids had several picnics during the five weeks which all enjoyed. She didn't know how long Tye would be around before leaving for his next assignment, but she knew one thing for sure, she was going to make the most of the time they had.

The telegraph she always dreaded came the next day. Tye opened it up and sat down at the table to read it.

Deputy U.S. Marshal Tye Watkins-Deputy U.S. Marshal Sam Jenkins

Fort Clark Texas

You will proceed to Bandera Texas to help Sheriff Henry "Buck" Hamilton with an explosive situation with several ranchers' problems with cattle rustlers. Possible range war developing STOP Keep me informed STOP

McMillan

U.S. Marshall Thomas Purnell

Western District-Austin, Texas

Tye folded up the telegram and looked at his wife. And started to say he was sorry but Rebecca held up her hand.

"Don't say anything, Tye," she said her voice trembling and tears welling up in her eyes. "Just go find Sam and I'll pack you some clothes and food."

Tye gave her a hug and a kiss on the cheek. He knew nothing he could say would make her feel any better. "I'll be back in a little while honey." He walked out the door to find Sam.

He had an idea where to find him when he wasn't in his quarters. He headed across the bridge into Brackett and Jim's Saloon. Tye didn't know the man well who had taken over the saloon after Jim was killed, but Major Thurston had told him he was running clean games as far as he knew and most of the soldiers went there. The previous owner, Jim, had been a good friend of Tye's before he was shot down. Tye had tracked the men down responsible for his death.

He heard Sam's laughter before he walked through the bat-winged doors of the saloon causing him to smile. Sam could laugh louder and longer over something, even a small thing, than anyone he had ever known.

Sam saw Tye as soon as the big man walked through the door. He also saw the piece of paper in his hand and knew the good times were probably over-at least for awhile.

"Come on over Tye," he hollered. Tye nodded and walked toward the table where Sam sat. He noticed as he walked past the bar it was polished and the glasses were sparkling clean. The floors were swept and the spittoons were clean and polished. He was impressed with the saloon. It didn't even stink-well, not much anyway. The owner couldn't do much with cowboys who didn't bathe regularly, but still it wasn't near as bad as most saloons he had been in.

"What's up," Sam asked as Tye sat down. Tye handed him the telegram. He read it and then reread it.

"Damn, wasn't we just there a month and half or so ago?"

Tye nodded. "Not exactly in the town itself but near enough." Tye took the beer the bartender brought over and took a good drink of the cool liquid. Wiping the foam from his mustache, he said, "It's late today so we'll head out early tomorrow. Should be there late the day after if we don't have any problems."

"What problems?"

"Haven't you heard about the Comanche?"

"Hell no. I've been drunk most part of the time we have been off," he chuckled and added, "recuperating from my wound you know." He laughed. "What trouble you talking about?"

"Thurston told me they were raiding farther south than normal under the leadership of Quanah Parker."

"Damn," Sam cursed. "He's a bad one. Had a friend killed by him and his bunch a couple years ago up north. They were hunting what was left of the buffalo when he and his outfit were attacked. Billy, that's was my friend, and six others were killed. Only two men escaped and they were both badly wounded."

Tye nodded. "There's no love lost between the Indians and the hide hunters." Tye finished his beer and stood up. "See you about daylight at the stables and bring some extra ammunition just in case and an extra canteen or two."

Sam watched his friend walk out and wondered why the extra canteens. Knowing Tye he has his reasons, he figured and went back to attacking the mug of beer in his hand.

The next morning just as the sun was peeking over the eastern horizon Tye and Sam were already few miles east of Fort Clark on the Old Mail Road that ran all the way to San Antonio. The road went west and north of Clark to Fort Davis and on to El Paso and all the way to San Diego, California.

"What the hell," Sam hollered as they saw a stage coming at them at a reckless speed and then they heard the rifle and pistol shots. Both men nudged there mount into a gallop and then reined in when the stage was a couple hundred yards away. They could see five or six Indians sixty or so yards behind the stage. Both men pulled their Henry's and moved to the side of the road so the stage could pass.

When the stage was almost to them they opened up with their Henrys. Both men being excellent shots and with mounts that would not flinch at the sound of rifle fire they knocked three off their ponies. The others, with one lying over his pony's neck, broke off the attack and headed back east on the road.

The stage had stopped about a hundred yards past the men and the two lawmen wheeled their mounts around and raced up to the stage.

The stage driver was off the stage kneeling beside a man lying in the dusty road on his back obviously wounded. When Tye and Sam road up the driver stood up.

"Tye Watkins!" he said loudly. "I thought that was you when we raced by you a minute ago. Never been so glad to see you in my life."

Tye dismounted and walked to the small, but wiry looking older man. "You okay Rufus you old geezer." He said shaking the man's hand. He looked at the stage and a frightened woman's face was peering out of the window and a man who looked more frightened than the woman was looking out the other. "Where did you pick up your friends, Tye asked nodding back down the road where the Indians lay sprawled on the hard ground?

"Bout three miles back down the road, "Rufus answered. "We came to the way station expecting to change our horses but they were under attack by a large group of Indians. We came on them sorter sudden like and I guess they didn't hear us with all the shooting going on. I heard the shooting afore I got there so I had the team running all out and was past them fore they realized we was even there. Six or so jumped on their ponies and took out after us. Old Bill there took one in the chest as he was firing over the top of the coach."

"He alive," Tye asked?

"Was…he died just after I laid him on the ground." He shook his head. "Been riding with James for nigh on three years. Was a good friend."

Tye looked at the man's face. "I had seen him on the stage with you before. Never knew his name though." He looked at the stage. "Everyone all right in there," he asked. The lady nodded her head. Tye looked at Sam. "Help me get James inside the stage." With this done he turned to Rufus. "Get on to Brackett and be sure you get a message to Major Thurston about this trouble. Sam and me are going to the station to see if we can help if we aren't too late.

Rufus shook his and Sam's hand. "Thank God you were out here on this road Tye. My horses were about done in and when James was hit his rifle fell off the coach. Onliest weapon we had left was mine and James's Colts."

"Just take it easy the rest of the way old timer," Tye said. As Tye and Sam mounted their horses Sam noted.

"That old man looks pretty tough."

Tye chuckled. "Yeah, he may have had only his Colt but those Indians would have their hands full if they had caught up with the coach." As they galloped past the Indians lying on the road Tye took a quick look at them and shouted, "Comanche."

Chapter Two

Ten minutes later the two lawmen could see smoke ahead but heard no gunfire which both knew wasn't a good sign. They slowed their mounts to a trot and pulled their Henry's from the leather. As they topped a small hill that was two hundred yards from the station they reined in and studied the situation over not wanting to run in half cocked and get their selves ambushed. They were too late to help the men who were at the station anyway so no use in getting in a situation where one or both of them could be killed.

After closely studying the area around the station both men nudged their mounts down the hill and into the yard. One man lay between the stable and the house and another in the doorway. The roof was on fire but the walls and inside the house wasn't. They knew the roof would cave in pretty quick so Tye ran into the house as Sam kept a look out. Tye came out dragging a man with one hand

and a woman with the other. He ran back in and brought out a teenage boy.

The man and woman were dead but the boy was still alive, but barely. He had not been scalped which to Tye meant he had put up a good fight and showed courage. Not scalping or disfiguring an enemy was a sign of respect by almost all Indians everywhere.

Tye splashed some water on the boys face and his eyes opened. Tye gave him some water which he drank greedily.

"My f…fo..folks?" he asked.

Tye shook his head and the boy closed his eyes as tears ran down his cheeks.

Suddenly his eyes flew open. "Lisa…did y..you f..find Elizabeth," he gasped.

"No we didn't son. Who is Elizabeth? Tye asked.

"M…my t..twin sister."He paused trying to get enough strength to continue. "Those d…de..devils must have to…took" he didn't finish. Tye shook his head and stood up. He walked outside and mounted Sandy. "Sam," he said looking at the roof. "See if you can find some blankets to wrap these people in before that roof caves in. I'm gonna scout around and see what direction the Comanche's went."

Sam found the blankets and had the people wrapped tight and a piece of rope he found in the stables that he cut and tied tight around the feet and above the head. He found a shovel also and was digging when Tye came back.

"What did you find?

"Headed south." He stepped down and took the shovel from Sam and started digging a second hole. The ground here was pretty rocky so the graves would be shallow and they would try and find enough big rocks close by to cover them and keep the varmints away.

"Sam," Tye said after scooping out a shallow grave and handing the shovel to his friend. "Remember awhile back when I told you about some outlaws that killed all my wife's mother's family except for a teenage boy named Todd."

Sam nodded. "I remember."

Todd stayed with the O'Malley's for awhile and I worked with him a lot: taught him how to fight, track and shoot, how to skin a deer and cure it so it could be used for clothes. I tried to teach him just about everything he needed to know to live out here and he was a quick learner He went back to the homestead to live and continue doing what his pa had done. They have a nice place; he has some cows, a few sheep, chickens, and just enough land to farm for one person to handle. There's deer and turkey a plenty in the area so I figured he will do okay, but there's a problem."

He had Sam's full attention. "What's that."

El Diablo

"If the Comanche continue the direction they are traveling they will hit his place." He paused for a moment. "Sam, I can't let that kid be killed without me at least trying to save him. I know we have orders, but I believe these changes things-at least for me it does. This is personal."

Sam caught Tye's drift as to where this conversation was headed. "You go and try to get him away before they hit his place and I'll get things started in Bandera with the sheriff. Just come as fast as you can." He reached back and opened one of his saddlebags and handed Tye a box of 44calibre shells for the Henry. "You may need these more than I do."

"Thanks Sam, Tye said taking the box and putting them into his saddlebag. He shook Sam's hand. "See you in a couple or so days." He reined Sandy around and headed south at a gallop.

Sam watched him ride away. He reached down and patted his horse's neck while he watched. "Be careful old friend," he mumbled out loud. "Be careful."

Tye's best guess from the tracks he was following was about forty or fifty Comanche. He was trotting Sandy and reached down and patted his neck. "One or two is a handful Sandy and man has to be crazy chasing forty or more by himself." Sandy nickered and Tye smiled. From the looks of the tracks he was no more than an hour behind them. Close enough to be watchful.

McMillan

Suddenly the sound of rifle fire came from in front of him and pretty close. He galloped for about a minute and halted Sandy. The gunfire had to be coming just over the hill in front of him so he dismounted and ran toward the top, getting on his belly just before reaching the crest of the hill and crawling the rest of the way to keep from sky lining himself.

The Comanche were milling around a homestead, some on their ponies and others on foot. Two men lay in the yard and a woman was being dragged out of the house. Tye watched and was grateful she appeared to be dead because he knew what would have happened if she hadn't been. He looked for the sister of the boy he had found earlier but saw no females anywhere except for the woman that was dragged from the homestead. He scooted back down the hill a ways and then ran to Sandy. This may be my chance to get around and ahead of them, he thought. They will be looting and scalping for a few minutes before setting the place on fire. He headed east as fast as Sandy could go to circle the homestead for a half mile and then headed south at an easy gallop.

About five miles from where he last saw the Comanche he came upon a ranch house, a large ranch house. Three men were in the corral breaking horses when he rode up. One man came out of the corral.

"Howdy, he said. He was an older man, probably in is late fifties or early sixties. Tye learned long ago that the sun, wind, and stress of living out here could make a man or woman appear older than they were. "What can I do for you"…he paused noticing the star on Tye's chest, "Marshal."

"You the owner of this ranch?"

"I am. Bill Wheeler's my name."

"Tye Watkins," Tye answered reaching down to shake the man's hand.

"From Clark?"

Tye nodded. "Listen Mr. Wheeler. There's about forty or so Comanche back there about four or five miles. They just killed a family of homesteaders and probably will continue this way."

"My God, "the man exclaimed. "That would be the Whitakers place." He turned to the men in the corral. "Mike, Cecil, come here quick." When the men arrived he introduced them to Tye and filled them in on what Tye had told him.

"How many men do you have Mr. Wheeler?"

"Six and two teenage sons that can shoot."

"Where are the others?"

Bill pointed and said about a mile or so that way rounding up some cattle.

"Can you get them here quick?"

Bill nodded. "Mike, get them and be quick about it"

"Yes sir, Mr. Wheeler," and ran to his horse a leaped into the saddle without using the stirrups.

"We need to make plans Bill," Tye said.

"Come into the house then." Before they entered the home Tye noted how well built it was. Thick adobe walls and a roof that had a foot of packed dirt and grass on top of the wooden roof.This place would be hard to burn he figured.

After introductions to the man's wife and sons they sat down. His two sons had heard a lot of stories from their father, soldiers that passed through on patrols and from drifting cowboys about Tye and his exploits and now he was here. They just stared.

"I take it you have plenty of ammunition and guns?' Bill Nodded. "Good, then here's the plan. Tell me if you agree or don't. You have a stout building close to the corrals. I can take thee of your men with me there and let two get in the loft above the barn. Let one in the house with you and your sons. When they ride in you can hit them from the front and with us at the building by the corral and the men in the loft we can get them in crossfire and maybe discourage them enough to go on their way."

"Sounds good to me, Tye" Bill said. "Martha, you gather up some rags, sheets, anything you can use as bandages. You boys get a little firewood and bring it in and get the fire in the stove going and put some water on. He walked over and took out two bottles of whiskey. "This will make good antiseptic," he said smiling.

El Diablo

Tye liked this man. He knew he had been down the river and up the creek as they say and was one tough hombre.

They heard the horses come into the yard and going to the door saw Mike and the men.

"Come in men," Bill said. He turned and went to a desk and opening the drawer took out several boxes of 44's and passed them to the men. He quickly explained to the men what Tye's plan was and they agreed it was the best one except for running like hell as the one called Buster said. They all laughed at the statement.

"Bill," Tye said. "We need to make things look normal so can one of your sons and the man who is going to stay in the house be in the yard chopping wood, raking, or anything to make things look okay. They will have a brave scouting out the place before they come in so let's get moving and get out of sight. You men in the loft take a canteen with you. It could be a long day."

Chapter Three

No more than fifteen minutes had passed when Tye saw the Comanche. He was almost a mile away and had topped a hill before seeing the ranch and immediately reined his pony around and out of sight. The three men with him stacked up to be the sort you want to be with in a fix like this where men were going to die. So were the men in the loft and the short time he was around Mike he knew he was. He figured Bill's sons were like their father so he had no worry there and Martha was like a hundred other frontier women he had met, strong and would stand by their man till the end.

He hoped his plan would work; kill enough of the Comanche to discourage them and realize whatever booty they could get here just wasn't worth it. He was looking north to the hill where he saw the Indian earlier but saw nothing. A covey of quail suddenly erupted from the stand of cedars and cactus just west of the building they were in. Tye whispered.

"One of you go to window behind us and keep a lookout to make sure they don't get behind us." He had barely gotten the words out when all hell broke loose.

The quiet was split wide open with the thunder of hooves and screaming Comanche's. Mike and the son who had been in the yard barely make it into the house as bullets were knocking out chunks of adobe all around the door and when the heavy wooden door slammed shut bullets and a couple arrows thudded into it. Rifles poked out the windows and accurate fire knocked four or five from their ponies. The two men in the loft opened up and knocked two or three more down. It was hard to see thru all the dust from the ponies but well enough for the men with Tye as they opened up and cut down a few more braves. Fire from the Comanche was raking the building where Tye and the men were but the walls were thick and none were getting through except through the window. Tye heard the fire from the man who had went to the window behind him and then a scream.

Tye turned just in time to see a Comanche pull his tomahawk from the man's head and jumped toward Tye. Tye used the Henry's barrel to block the blow intended for his head and then hit the warrior flush in the face with his fist. The man stumbled back to the wall and slid down it unconscious. One of the men beside Tye had seen what happened and shot the Indian in the chest.

McMillan

It was over as quickly as it had started. The Comanche was gone. The dust and the smoke hung in the air for a few minutes. No one moved. Then Tye walked out of the building and looked around. He saw nothing but dead men and a couple of dead horses.

Eleven braves lay in the dust and one in the building. As he walked among the men on the ground making sure they were dead he heard a groan and quickly was beside the wounded warrior. He had a crease above his right ear and had been knocked unconscious. Bill came out and his two sons and stood by Tye. Bill started to raise his Colt but Tye stopped him. The two men who had been with Tye in the building came out carrying the third man who had been killed. One of Bills sons had been nicked in the shoulder.

"Why didn't you let me just shoot the red bastard?"

"Listen to me all of you. The Indian, whether Apache, Comanche, or whatever, respects bravery like all of you showed here today. They also respect a man's honor. I am going to help this man up and bandage his wound. I want him to watch each of you as you carry his dead friends out of the yard and lay them gently on the ground and I do mean gently. Then I'm going to take him to the others and let them see we are men of honor like they are."

"But they savages Tye," Mike said. "They a...he was cut off by Tye's words.

El Diablo

"They are not savages Mike. They are men fighting for their way of life. All the Indians I have ever known just wanted to live the way their forefathers had-free. We are running them off the land they have roamed for generations. We have killed off their main source of food and clothing, the buffalo. If you were in their place you would be doing the same as they are."

Mike and the others were looking at the ground not saying anything, just taking in what Tye had said. Martha came out with hot water and bandages. She cleaned the wound and wrapped his head. The Indian watched as the men begin carefully carrying the dead outside the yard and laying them gently on the ground.

"Bill," Tye said looking at the rancher. "I need a horse to give to this man. A gift from you to a fellow warrior. Make a big show of it when you give him the reins."

Bill started to protest but Tye said. "I promise you if you do this you will never have another problem with the Comanche."

Bill looked at Tye like he was crazy and started to argue, but then thought better of it turned around and walked to the corral. A minute later he came back leading a horse. Tye had asked Mike to round up as many of the Comanche ponies as they could and they had come back with five.

Bill put on a show of giving the reins of the horse to the Comanche who was hesitate to take the reins at first. When he did Tye could tell he was confused at what was going on. He figured the warrior was expecting to be killed not treated for his wound and now…a horse given to him. He was probably thinking what kind of crazy people are these anyway. Tye Smiled and motioned for him to mount the horse which he did.

Tye mounted Sandy and with Mikes help gathered the other ponies and headed the direction the Indians had went when the fight was over. They had traveled a little over a mile from the ranch when they saw the Indians. Tye turned to the wounded man and motioned for him to go. He rode away but looking frequently over his shoulder like he was expecting to be shot. He had the dead Indians ponies following him.

Mike started to turn to go back but held up as Tye grabbed him by the arm.

"Just wait a minute Mike," Tye said. "You might just learn something." As he spoke a single warrior rode toward them on a beautiful solid black pony. Watching the man come toward them Tye was amazed at the man's size. *He has to be over six foot tall and has one hell of a body to go with the height.* His coal black hair hung loosely down to his shoulders and he had a single eagle feather woven into it. On top of everything else he was strikingly handsome for an Indian. Tye then knew who he was-Quanah Parker himself. He was suddenly a little concerned because he had heard of this man's hatred for the white man.

"Don't make a stupid move Mike," he said in just over a whisper. That's the he wolf himself, Quanah Parker.

Tye raised his hand, palm out, in a show of friendship when the warrior was twenty feet away. Quanah did the same and Tye relaxed some. They stared at each other for a moment before Quanah spoke in surprisingly good English.

Running Elk told me what you did for him. It was a good thing not to kill him."

"There had been enough killing and we saw no need for more Quanah Parker."

Quanah sat up even straighter. "You know who I am?"

"Everyone knows of the great War Chief of the band of Quahadi of the Comanche Nation. It is an honor to meet you."

Quanah looked at this white man, probably the biggest he had ever seen and there was something else about him but he wasn't able to put a finger on it. He felt he knew this man. "You have a name?"

Tye nodded. "Tye Watkins."

A smile came across the chief's face. "I have heard of you and now we meet-two warriors. Let us talk and he dismounted and sat on the ground. Tye dismounted and handed Sandy's reins to Mike who remained mounted.

"Your warriors that were killed are ready for you to take with you and give them the proper burial of a Comanche warrior," Tye said.

"Running Elk told me this and also you and the others treated them with respect." He nodded. "This is good." He paused for a moment. "I have heard you are like Apache and have respect for the Redman and our way of life."

"I do respect the Redman. If I was born Indian I would be as you and the Apache, and other tribes and would be fighting the white man for what they are doing to my way of life."

Quanah nodded. "It is good to talk to a white man who understands the Redman and why he is fighting so hard to keep his way of life that has been for generations." He stood up and Tye did also. He reached out with his hand and Tye did also as they each clasped the others wrist. "It is good between us and I hope we do not meet in battle. I think I would not like to kill you," he said smiling.

"Nor I you," Tye said smiling also. This brought another smile to Quanah's face.

Quanah jumped on his pony's back. "We will gather our dead." He turned his pony and rode back to the others.

Tye mounted Sandy and said. "Lets go back to the ranch and see what happens."

El Diablo

A few minutes later they arrived back to an anxious group of men.

"What happened," Bill Asked.

"You ain't gonna believe this Bill," Mike said leaping from his horse."We just met the top he wolf of all the Comanche, Quanah Parker his own self. Sat right down with him had us a good palaver we did.

Tye didn't say anything. He just let the cowboy talk. "He had heard of Tye and they talked to each other like old friends. Said Tye understood the Indian and he respected that. Said he was coming to collect his dead an…"

"Here they come," the oldest of Bills sons said. They all looked in the direction he was pointing and saw the thirty or so warriors coming down the hill toward the ranch yard.

"Don't do anything stupid like go for a gun," Tye said sharply. They were ready though just in case. They watched as the warriors dismounted and placed the dead on the horses that Tye had brought back to them plus others they had caught up with. As the white men watched, Quanah walked his pony a few steps toward them and then Running Elk came up beside him and Quanah handed him something. Running Elk rode his pony into the yard and dismounted and walked directly to Martha and handed her the object. Tye smiled. It was a peace pipe and beautifully carved and stained with different colors. He smiled at

Martha and then looked at Tye and nodded. He walked back to his mount and rode back to the others. They left but as they rode away Quanah hung back and turned his mount back toward the ranch and the white men. He raised his arm with the peace sign. Tye raised his and was happy to see the others do the same.

"Well I be damned," Bill said. "Can you believe that?"

"This is absolutely beautiful," Martha said holding the pipe up.

"It's a peace pipe Mrs. Wheeler. Ya'll won't be bothered by the Comanche any more. Apaches and bandits maybe," Tye said laughing, "but not the Comanche."

"I tell you Tye," Bill said shaking his head, "I thought you were a little tetched in the head when you said to treat and release that Comanche. Just goes to show how much I know," he added laughing.

"I think we all learned some things today because like you Bill, I thought Tye was a little crazy too," Mike said. Everyone laughed.

"I've got to be riding Bill," Tye said reaching out to shake the man's hand. "Sorry for your loss," he said nodding toward the hand that had been killed.

"Larry was a good and loyal hand. He was also a friend, but I'll tell you this if you had not come when you did we would all be dead and scalped by now."

El Diablo

"Amen to that," Mike said.

Martha came out of the house after putting away the pipe. "Tye Watkins," She said her hands on her hips and her chin out. "You will do no such thing as leave this late in the day. I will fix the best vittles you ever had and you will sleep here tonight and I won't take no for an answer," she said in tone that had a lot authority to it.

Tye started to say something but Bill waved his hand and said laughing, "You heard the boss, Tye and if there's one thing I've learned over the last twenty years is when she says jump, I ask how high."

"Looks like I have no choice," Tye said smiling.

"You don't," Martha said as she turned and walked back into the house. She stopped and turned back to the men. "Ya'll get poor Larry buried and all of you will eat in the house tonight. The two sons were ecstatic, Tye was staying. They wanted to hear stories from this man who was becoming a legend in this part of the country. The men, though wanting to say it aloud, wanted to spend a little time with this man also and were happy they didn't have to eat their own cooking tonight.

Two hours later after eating a meals of beef steaks, fried potatoes, cabbage and corn the men sat on the porch smoking. This was the time James, the youngest son of Bill had been waiting for

"Mr. Watkins," James said, "We've heard stories about you from drifting cowboys and sometimes soldiers from Fort Clark when they stop by on patrol about you ever since I can remember. Are they true like the one about your fighting Apaches since you were eight years old?"

Tye chuckled. No, I sure a lot of them are stretched a mite as to what really happened, but I've had a pretty exciting life so far. To answer your question I was fourteen when I killed my first Apache with a knife."

"With a knife?" Mike exclaimed.

Tye nodded."There were two of them on my pa and I came running to help and jumped on one their backs and cut his throat. Pa killed the other one with his knife. I didn't have what one would say was a normal childhood. There were no close neighbors and my only friend was an Apache boy about my own age. I found him one day with a broken leg and helped him to our house where pa set the bone and ma bandaged him up. We became friends after that and I spent time at his Rancheria and he at my home. This was before all the trouble started between the whites and the Apache. We stayed close till the trouble started about four years later and the warriors would not let him visit any more. I didn't see him for years until we met in battle one day. It was the worst day of my life. We ended up facing each other in hand to hand fight with knives. I didn't want to kill him nor did he want to kill me or at least I was hoping he didn't. It didn't work out that way though and I had to kill him or he would have me."

"My pa, Ben, had been a trapper or what the writers of the dime novels called, a mountain man, for years before coming to Texas and meeting ma. He trapped with Jim

Bridger and Shakespeare McDovitt and some other trappers I'm sure you have heard or read about."

"I read a couple about Ben," James said. "Never thought about him being your pa though."

"No reason for you too," Tye said. "From the time I could walk Ben was teaching me to read the tracks of animals. When I was eight or nine I was learning how to fight with my fist, knives, tomahawks, and guns. I practiced every day of my youth learning the ins and outs of fighting and everything Ben knew about survival. I'm still learning something every day."

"Why did you quite scouting for the army and take up marshaling," the boy asked.

"James, why don't you run along to bed and quite pestering Tye with all these questions, Bill said.

"It's okay Bill. I don't mind and how can a boy learn if he don't ask questions," he chuckled. "You may not know this but the Apache respected me as a fellow warrior. I could track like them, I thought the way they did, and could fight like them so they made me a hunted man. Sorter put me on a wanted list like we do by putting out posters on men wanted for robbery etc. This went on for years and I suddenly had a family and was chasing Apaches who wanted me dead. I figured it would be safer chasing outlaws but," he chuckled, "As you saw today I just can't seem to get away from Indians."

"You ever been shot?"

"More times than I can count," Tye said laughing. "Been shot with bullets, arrows, stabbed and clubbed." He laughed and added. "Old sawbones at the forts hospital said I'll never die because I have no vital organs."

Mike had a question. "Today's fight with the Comanche anything like a fight with the Apache?"

Tye thought for a moment. "Sometimes, but the Apache doesn't have the numbers like the Sioux or the Comanche or a number of other tribes. The Apache is probably, and I'm basing this mostly on what my pa told me because he fought many different tribes, the fiercest and best warriors of the lot. They use hit and run tactics: world's best at ambushing their enemy. I always tell people that being on patrol chasing Apaches is days of boredom and a few minutes of sheer terror. Seldom does a fight last more than a few minutes even though it may seem a lot longer.

"What's it like Tye?" Bill asked. "I mean being ambushed or in a hand to hand fight with Apaches?"

"Like I said, sheer terror especially when they overrun your position and it becomes hand to hand because the soldiers for the most part aren't good knife fighters. You hear the screams of men being shot, knifed, or tomahawked to death. You hear the whinnying of wounded horses. You hear the all too familiar 'thunk' of a bullet striking flesh or a head being split open, and it becomes hard to see and breathe because of all the smoke from the guns. But I think the worse is the smell of blood and death all around you. It's not pleasant Bill and if you haven't seen it before the one today, and today wasn't anything like most Apache fights, I hope you don't."

James said. "You said sheer terror. Surely you don't mean you being scared."

"Sure I'm scared going into a fight where another man is trying to kill you. A man is crazy or a liar if he says he is not but it's how you handle that fear, James. I've seen them all-men who are so scared they can't move when the fight comes and they usually get themselves and some of their friends killed. I've seen men who are screaming they are so scared but they perform like they are supposed to do and others I know are scared but you would never know it. Yeah James, I get scared just like everyone else but it's just a matter of overcoming that fear and doing your job, doing what you have to do to save yourself and your friends." Tye stood up and said over his shoulder as he walked to the corral. "Be back in a minute. I'm gonna check on Sandy."

"Now there walks a man," Bill said to his two sons. "He's becoming a legend out here but I could tell he doesn't care too much about talking about himself. I think that's why he's checking on his horse just to get the conversation about something else or someone else."

Mike spoke up. "I was so scared today when we went to where the Comanche's were I almost wet my pants." Everyone laughed. "I was scared but there was old Tye just a sitting on his horse as calm as could be watching and knowing what they were going to do because I wanted to get the hell away and he held me back and told me I was going to learn something. I was really nervous when the biggest damn Injun I ever did see came riding up to us on that coal black pony and Tye just a sitting there. And then when Tye said it was Quanah Parker himself I think I did wet my pants a little." More laughter from the others followed that statement. "Then when Tye told him his name you could tell it meant something to him. Not too sure he didn't feel a little fear himself," he said chuckling out loud."

Tye came back. Bill asked. "I never asked you Tye but why was you down here anyway?"

"Just south of here about five or so miles is a homestead where my nephew is living."

"You mean the Jenkins kid," Mike asked?

Tye nodded. "His mother was my ma's sister."

"They were good people," Bill said, "It was a tragedy what happened, but young Todd has stepped in and has the place looking real good."

"Figured he would, Tye replied. "I was headed there to warn him about the Comanche, but they are headed back north now so I'll go meet my partner in Bandera. We have a rustling ring to try and break up before a full scale range war breaks out"

Bill nodded. "I've heard a little about it from a friend of mine who is one of the ranchers losing stock."

'Who would that be?" Tye asked.

El Diablo

"James Fowler, owner of the Lazy B Ranch. Kno'd him for years and he's as straight as the day is long. Hope you can help him out of the problem he's having."

"We're going to do our best, Bill. I saddled Sandy just now so I think I'll be heading toward Bandera to catch up with Sam, my partner."

"I thought you were spending the night and leaving in the morning."

"Was, but got to thinking I could be half way there by then". He chuckled and said, "Don't want my partner to get into trouble you know. He's a good man but sometimes lets his temper cloud his judgment. He stepped into the saddle and reached down and shook Bill's and the others hands. Ya'll take care and if you see the Jenkins boy tell him I said hello."'

"Well do that Tye and again thanks," Bill said. Tye turned Sandy and headed out of the yard toward Bandera and to what he figured toward new trouble.

McMillan

El Diablo

McMillan